The Rantings of Love

Ericka Lynn

Mountain Hood Books-Beaverton, OR
ISBN: 978-0-578-74257-1
Library of Congress Control Number: 2020915451
Title: The Rantings of Love
Author: Ericka Lynn
Digital distribution | 2020
Paperback | 2020

Dedication

Thank you to all of life's ups and downs, the struggles and the fears, and the relationships that inspired me to write this book. Here's to the imperfections of life, and those that boldly accept them.

Cassandra savored the aroma of chai tea as it trickled warm and inviting down her throat. She didn't know much about the mission, but she knew it would be taking Brandon away from her for a year. *A year*, she contemplated. That was 12 drill weekends, 70 boxing classes, 52 trash days, 8 haircuts, 4 oil changes…and countless nights without him in her arms. She closed her eyes. The crisp autumn air swept across her face as she imagined Brandon's arms wrapped tightly around her. It would be a year before it would be that way again.

A year seemed like such an impossibility, and right now Cassandra didn't even know if she had the strength to make it through the weekend. The babysitter would be there for another couple of hours, maybe she would distract herself with a haircut. She had caught Brandon staring when she cut it for the first time, and all she could remember was a softness to his face as he breathed, "Nice haircut by the way." Then there was the airport, the planning conference and their final training event. Cassandra played these clips over and over in her head like a movie trailer. Memories were all she had to keep her company while he was gone. On the nights leading to the deployment she held onto after work drinks, coffee and football games. The promise of being together carried her through the mobilization ceremony. She sighed. She really didn't know how she would do life without him.

Cassandra sat parked in the driveway. Little people would be unrelenting, and she would need to prepare for the emotional onslaught she knew was coming the minute she walked in the door. She took a breath and swung it open. Above the cheers and clapping, Cassandra strained to hear updates on the kids' behavior. Heather threw tantrums all morning and was finally taking a nap…Hunter built skyscrapers out of Play Doh… both were freshly changed or had just used the potty…neither of them had anything to eat all morning except chicken nuggets.

Chicken nuggets. Some of the best moments of her life involved chicken nuggets, and crawling around Brandon's house to retrieve them. french fries sprinkled the floor like confetti, and Cassandra smiled as her thoughts drifted to her and Brandon darting around on all fours to beat party production. He had a great smile, something she carried with her wherever she went. There were few things in life that a Brandon smile couldn't fix. A frown tugged at the edges of her mouth, as she wondered if this might be one of them.

The hours ticked along and somehow Cassandra made it to bed time. With two little people fast asleep, soon only she remained. *Only 321 days to go,* she contended. She wrapped her arms around her pillow, imagining Brandon lying next to her. What she wouldn't give to hold him one last time.

Yet Cassandra often paid a tax for loving Brandon. Payment generally came in the form of threatening text messages and intense accusations. They were often paired with demands for increased child support, changes in custody and revoked "permission" to co-parent. It was just like their marriage. No one would have blamed her if she really had been driven into the arms of another man, except that wasn't entirely true. She wasn't so much driven as she was pushed, and David had been the one to give her the final shove.

***

David languished on the frame of the bedroom door, claiming gastrointestinal issues as his latest health crisis. The grimace on his face and doubled over posture suggested this was probably true, but Cassandra could do without the dramatic gestures. At the news, she offered only a mildly sympathetic, "That's too bad," and turned back towards the computer. She needed something to occupy her and the children's day now that their schedule seemed to be wide open.

It was the fourth of July, the barbeque she had been looking forward to all week was likely off. David crouched next to her as she turned to shield her disappointment. "I want you and the kids to have fun today. Go do whatever you want." Hunter had been asking about the carousel since they moved almost a year ago. It would easily take half the day. Anything to take her mind off of the life that was in front of her. She gathered coats and shoes and wondered what the going rate was for total surgeries in one marriage. She wondered if this last one had set a new record.

With the final click of the seatbelt, Cassandra put the truck on cruise control and did the same with her mind. She needed to get out. The last few years felt like four seasons of winter. How long it would be before spring would come, was anyone's best guess. The last four years had been a blur. Stomach surgeries, knee surgeries, back surgeries, her own C-section recovery. The birth of her two children, the new duty assignment, the new house, having to pass a physical fitness test to keep her job. The unexpected death of her father had hit her the hardest.

Life went along, until it didn't. It started in small imperceptible stages. *I'm tired. I need some time to myself. I need a break from the kids*. Cassandra often echoed David's sentiments with the added bonus of lamenting motherhood and a career. Sympathy was not something she routinely received. Instead, dirty diapers, a messy kitchen and constant complaints were her reward. She often wondered if relationships and raising kids was just hard and she lacked the tools to do the job properly. She had her faith, but she didn't seem to be very good at that either. Maybe she just didn't know how to do life.

For years Cassandra prayed. She prayed for the direction of her marriage. She prayed for the medical restoration of her husband. She prayed for her own peace of mind and strength. Her consistency often made up for David's deficit. Yet life remained largely unchanged, until God sent her Brandon.

She remembered the first time she met Brandon Fletcher. Everything about him was intense; his eyes, his voice and his mannerisms. At first small talk consisted of complaints about people, about things and about their moral character. His anger was overwhelming, and Cassandra wasn't sure how much of her job description was supposed to involve excessive complaining. If they didn't have to work together, she wasn't entirely convinced she would have invested in him. Yet despite Cassandra's disinterest in conflict, Brandon seemed to gravitate toward her controlled optimism.

He sent phone calls, emails, and even offered to watch her children after her father died. He had shared Christmas and Easter with Cassandra and David, and was beginning to become the friend she had prayed so desperately for. In one tear choked conversation she confessed her reservations about David's upcoming surgery and the affect she feared it would have on their lives. She held her breath as she uttered her last tear choked sentence. Brandon really didn't do sentiment and Cassandra thought perhaps she had said too much. He sighed, then paused before offering, "I don't always know what to say, but I am here if you need to talk. I am here anytime you need me."

In the months that followed Cassandra watched as the guarded layers of Brandon's own life began to crumble. He started to confide in her his own feelings of frustration and overwhelm with their impending brigade level exercise. At one point he finally awarded her the title of *friend*, and even began to reach out to David with shared interests.

Cassandra's thoughts were interrupted with protests from the back seat. The temple over her right eye began to throb. She just wanted one drama free trip and immediately lamented the decision to travel so far outside her normal commuting distance by herself. With each passing exit, her desire to abort the mission continued to grow. Maybe she would just turn around. Maybe David really was better at this than she was. The next exit was theirs. Maybe she would just take it and see what happened.

Carnival music and the smell of popcorn poured through the windows as they pulled into the parking lot. The whining ceased, and soon Hunter and Heather forgot all about their reasons for being unhappy. Painted horses and windy slides seemed to be the magical potion for contentment. Cassandra breathed a sigh of relief as she offered alternating sips of her rainbow flavored snow cone. She looked affectionately at Hunter as he took toddler sized bites of his hotdog and popcorn. In that moment it was just her and the kids. She felt the stress and anxiety wash away with each sip of her slushy oasis. She needed this, but in the back of her mind wondered how long the feeling would last. She knew what was waiting for her back home, and was in no hurry to get there. She checked her phone. No response yet.

The magic began to wane and Cassandra knew it was her cue to go. She grabbed their bags and loaded everyone in the stroller, hoping to avoid the meltdown she knew was coming. They barely made it to the truck before tired began to exude from every part of their tiny bodies. Cassandra hoisted them into the back seat and turned on the music. They were both asleep before she left the parking lot. She breathed a deep sigh of relief. Now if only he would answer his phone…

Woodburn was the point of no return, and if Cassandra didn't hear back soon, she would be faced with a decision. She wondered if there was any truth in David's statements. 5 miles, 3 miles, 2 miles…Maybe God didn't want to authorize her plan and they should just head home. Cassandra closed in on the final mile when the familiar *ding* of her cell phone sounded. She turned just in time to make the exit. A secondary *ding* sounded. She would need to delay 20 minutes. Cassandra looked over her shoulder as she pulled into the *McDonald's* parking lot. Little arms and legs began to flail, and not a moment too soon.

Brandon answered the door with a smile as he ushered Cassandra and his tiny visitors inside. The kids raced through the door, running and shouting from wall to wall. Cassandra eyed the sparse furnishings, wondering how often he entertained guests. Surveying the adult sized barstools, she placed the Happy Meals on the floor and began to unpack their contents. She admittedly felt a little weird being in his house, but he had come to visit her and David on several occasions and she was simply returning the favor. She glanced at him over her shoulder as he smiled warmly in her direction. Cassandra turned away with a shy grin. She wasn't used to having people notice her.

Out of the corner of her eye, Cassandra saw chicken nuggets and french fries fly across the floor and instinctively knelt down to pick them up. She was on the verge of apologizing when she looked up to find Brandon at eye level with his own collection of half eaten treasures. She thoughtfully grinned. Being a human vacuum cleaner was a task she often performed solo. Cassandra stood to discard the remnants when she caught a whiff of something slightly off. She sighed and followed Brandon to the kitchen to retrieve a plastic bag. She might as well do both of them while she was at it. She threw the bag outside and washed her hands before handing Heather a drink.

Brandon's eyes followed her back to the kitchen as she helped herself to a glass of water. He smiled with a sweetness that suggested he liked the way she looked there. He joined her moments later and asked if she would like some coffee. Cassandra shook her head. She didn't actually like coffee, even though it was her activity of choice among friends. Many a conversation were started with a cup of fresh brew. With his newly poured mug, the conversation was officially open for business.

Chicken nuggets continued to fly through the air as Brandon ducked a near miss, playfully wrestling Hunter and Heather to the ground. Hunter squealed in delight and ran off before emphatically petitioning, "Again!" Between impromptu tickle fests, Brandon focused his attention back to her. Cassandra paused as she silently wondered when the last time she noticed David playing that way with the children. If she were being honest with herself, she wondered when the last time David noticed *her* like that. Most days he seemed disinterested in what she had to say and didn't even look at her. He would often blame it on the distraction of the kids or his latest medical ailment. Cassandra often wondered if he was even capable of giving her the attention she needed.

Heather and Hunter's squeals began to subside and Cassandra knew her welcome would be short lived. She looked out the window and asked "Do you want to go to the park with us?"

"Sure, just let me get my shoes." Her eyes followed Brandon across the floor as he unzipped his hooded sweater. She watched as he slipped it off, revealing a white tank top stretched tightly across his chest. Catching her gaze out of the corner of his eye, Brandon paused long enough to square his shoulders towards her. Cassandra inhaled sharply, scrambling to focus on his face. It had been a while since she had seen a man without a shirt, at least one like that. If Brandon was noticing her, she was sure he was noticing her reaction. He smiled sheepishly before retrieving his shoes and shirt from the other room.

Once at the park, she continued to notice him. She noticed the way he chased Hunter up the slide and the way he picked him up to make a basket. She noticed the effort he made to engage a grumpy Heather, and noticed how he alternated playing with the children to sit next to her in conversation. Despite the complex topics, she noticed how light and easy the conversation flowed. Meaningful discussions were another area Cassandra was often deficient in. She soaked them in like a plant soaking in the sun's rays. Her energy tank was almost full and she silently wondered why every day couldn't be like this.

The afternoon began to slip away and Cassandra knew she would have to head home soon. Brandon walked her to the truck and helped her settle the kids. She thanked him for the day and offered her usual hug. As she lifted her arms around his shoulders, he put his arms over the top of hers and pulled her in tight. With nowhere left to place her face, she turned it sideways and rested it on his chest as his heartbeat echoed in her ear. The needle of her energy tank surged all the way to the right and a smile enveloped her face. Hugs were her favorite, and this one was especially comforting. She felt the worries of the last five years wash away and breathed a deep sigh of contentment. Cassandra couldn't remember the last time she felt so at ease. David didn't hug her like that, and when he did she felt it more of an obligation than an expression of affection. Even still, she didn't know if she should enjoy hugging someone who wasn't her husband. She pulled away and felt her energy tank flicker. The surge was real. He felt safe. Maybe just one more hug to get her home so she could face reality.

Cassandra rode a tidal wave of energy all the way home, and even a still languishing David had little effect on her. The dankness of the downstairs living space where he spent most of his time threatened to suck her in, but Cassandra opted to attend the neighbors' barbeque potluck despite having nothing prepared to share. Engaging in small talk with strangers did not bother her in the least, at least not today. Children's ages, occupations, neighborhood traditions, it was all relative. Soon fireworks would commence, and Cassandra would give Hunter and Heather an age appropriate send off.

After the children were in bed, Cassandra thought back to her hug that afternoon with Brandon. She wondered why David didn't hug her like that. She wondered why he didn't look at her when she spoke. She wondered why he seemed so disinterested in her day. Despite her battery surging day with Brandon, she wanted every day to be like that, and she wanted it be like that with David. Cassandra couldn't recall a time when their relationship embodied such affection, and wondered if such a thing could be taught. Maybe with enough effort David could learn to love her, just like she had learned to love him.

She wanted to spend more time with David and didn't want to be the first one he complained to. She wanted to be on the same page with the children and wanted him to show an interest in her. She wanted more intimacy and wanted him to touch her. She wanted him to notice her like she was his wife instead of a live in babysitter.

The changes started small and grew incrementally. Having dinner ready when she got home. Putting limits on his "me" time so he could spend time with her once the kids were in bed. Asking how her day went. He even offered to have sex with her when she petitioned. But after a couple of weeks of thoughtful action, David determined Cassandra's tank was full and no further action would be required. Yet to Cassandra, he was barely scratching the surface. If this was all the effort he was capable of, it wasn't enough. Her heart sank as she realized that either David did not want to meet her needs, or lacked the ability to do so. Either option drained the last of her residual tank and sent her into a season of despair. She was about to start her month long military training on empty, a prospect David was seemingly okay with.

***

It was day two. Starkly similar to day one, but day two didn't start with seeing Brandon's face. "This is going to be a long year," Cassandra moaned as she pulled herself out of bed. It was Sunday, but at least there was church to provide a distraction. Church would afford her an hour and a half of kid free time to regain her sanity. Cassandra always liked church, and extended the invitation to Brandon on many occasions. When it seemed he was close to conceding, he recanted with rallies against organized religion and the evils it plagued upon society. Even still, she felt a strong Brandon vibe whenever she was there. She could see him sitting in the chair next to her, rocking out to nonjudgmental contemporary worship.

Faith was the only thing besides Brandon that was getting Cassandra through the energy crisis. Now that Brandon was gone, faith was all she had left. She often wondered if she was able to invest as much faith in God as she did in Brandon. There was a time when faith emerged as the single most important thing in her life, but that was before there were children. That was before all of the surgeries. That was before Cassandra entered safe mode. That was a lifetime ago. She wanted someone to walk along side her in faith. These days she was doing well to do any of the walking herself.

She often wondered how it would look if she were to walk into church with someone new. Would they think less of her? Did she have a certain grace period to remain single, or did people just pretend like her divorce never happened? Cassandra thought back to life pre divorce, remembering the pastor's wife coming to check on her after David's social media fallout. He had checked himself into a program for depression and later converted to Islam. Cassandra had born the weight of his decisions and was ready to receive her tongue lashing. Instead, she was met with an unexpected understanding and empathy as the pastor's wife stated, "Obviously we would like you to stay together, but we understand if you can't." So that was it. No recanting of scripture passages, no guilt, no attempt at mandated reconciliation.

Cassandra received similar support from the volunteers that ran the church daycare, as well as from other mothers in the congregation. The pastor's wife even went out of her way to create a Growth Group tailored to Cassandra's child care needs. Despite their on demand schedule, both the pastor and his wife came to visit her home on several occasions to see how the transition was going. Each time they came equipped with side dishes and a listening ear. Even then Cassandra was spared the preachiness she thought her life decision warranted, and was met with what appeared to be unconditional acceptance.

Acceptance was not something Cassandra was used to receiving, in church, or anywhere else. That was the very thing that drew her to this church to begin with. More than a quaint motto, *No perfect people allowed* seemed to actually be a perception people lived by. The more she interacted with them, the more she realized the version she saw on Sunday was the same version that existed throughout the week and in life. A church without an agenda was puzzling to her.

In one of his sermons, the pastor recanted, "If telling someone else the gospel does not help them, then you're not doing it right." *The gospel helping people in their day to day lives*. Cassandra had never heard of such things. Religion and the Bible were tools to teach on a Sunday morning. Sure they may cheer you up, but never on purpose. You had to be in the right mood to learn something. Even then, it was spiritual platitudes and positive mantras that briefed well, but did not actually hold up against the elements. Cassandra contemplated this strange new concept as she relived the events of the last few months. The pastor and his wife reaching out. People coming forward to check in on her and include her in their activities. Sending her a friend when she was in dire need of one. Maybe the pastor was right, maybe he really was on to something. Maybe love and acceptance were the only mission you were supposed to have.

Her thoughts naturally shifted back to Brandon. She had been different with him. She didn't show him her whole self, at least not all at once, and at least not the self-destructive pieces. Those parts weren't conducive to his personality so she kept them to herself. Often hours would pass between phone calls or text messages as she re-digested her hurtful comments, repackaging them in a more constructive manner. Such comments wouldn't have been helpful for Brandon, and Cassandra gradually learned they weren't helpful to most people. She still had a hard time accepting unconditional love, but maybe through Brandon, she could show herself what it was supposed to look like. Maybe the gospel really did have prevalence in her life after all.

Cassandra returned from church to a text from Brandon. He was on his way to the mobilization site and just wanted her to know he read her letter.

Cassandra's heart quickened as she imagined him reading her letter right before getting on the airplane. She loved that man, and the smallest part of her was beginning to think that maybe he loved her too. She wondered if love would be enough to get her through the next year, or if she would need something entirely different.

***

Cassandra lost track of the days. All she knew was that it was day eight million and fourteen of misery. The woodland fires, the excessive heat, the assortment of battle gear that had to be worn, all of it contributed to the collective suck. People were yelling, they were upset, they were angry and all of it was directed at her. She was the Support Operations Officer; it was her fault the training was not going according to plan. In honor of the eight millionth and fourteenth day of training, Cassandra marked the occasion by silently sulking. Earlier on she had vocalized her frustrations to others, swelling up to ten times her normal size to let them know that she would not be taking their crap. She was done. She was tired. All she wanted to do was crawl inside her sleeping bag and disappear. Maybe they could stage a kidnapping for her to be worked into the mock wartime write up. Maybe she could be a casualty at the front gate, taken prisoner by enemy forces. Maybe she would be KIA and it would finally put an end to this drama not on daytime television. Maybe someone could rescue her from this training and she wouldn't have to play this ridiculous game anymore.

Underneath her Kevlar helmet Cassandra saw Brandon glancing at her out of the corner of her eye. She was riding with her favorite person, and all she could focus on was the growing dissatisfaction inside of her. They just returned from the ammo handling point, her favorite place within the whole exercise, and still her spirits remained low. Cassandra couldn't pinpoint the source of disappointment. All she knew was that it must really be something if its presence masked her present company. She could tell Brandon was searching for any clue that might snap her out of her current malaise. She appreciated his concern, but she had to conserve what little energy she had. She couldn't let anyone in. Not tonight.

Their HMMWV rolled into camp and Brandon hopped out to secure it against the August night. Real or imagined, enemy precautions always had to be taken. He looked at her with a combination of concern and defeat as Cassandra averted her eyes. She knew there was nothing he could do to improve her mood and there was no need to bring him down with her. "I'm just going to go. I'll talk to you later."

As she turned to walk away, Brandon grabbed her arm, affirming, "Your hug meter is low," and pulled her in close. "You were there for me last night, so I will be here for you tonight." The needle on Cassandra's hug meter flickered as Brandon rested his chin on her forehead. Interpersonal communication was not this thing, but for her, Cassandra saw he was willing to make an effort. She let her stress disappear in the safety of the darkness and his arms before she made the long trek across the field to her tent. Her hug metered pulsed as she laid out her sleeping bag and prepped for the next day's mission. It pulsed as she wiped down her weapon for the morning ambush. It continued to pulse as she made her way back across the empty field and found her way to his command post door. She was ready to talk now, she hoped the invitation was still open.

Brandon saw her hesitation and walked her outside. He studied her face then gestured to the nighttime sky. He recounted facts about the constellations; frequency, type and name. He toted his own passion for astronomy and his fascination of the unknown. Cassandra sat in revered silence as tears streamed down her face. Her frustrations were reaching their limit. The training exercise. David's latest surgery. The stress of going home. The future of her marriage. She had received words of encouragement from a few others during the exercise, but somehow she needed a perspective only Brandon could offer.

"It sounds like you've already made your decision," he stated softly. The tone of his voice matched the softness of his moonlit face. In her heart Cassandra knew he was right. Yet she wasn't sure she could bring herself to do it, not again. As if reading her thoughts, Brandon continued, "It may not be today, it may not be tomorrow, it may not even be two weeks from now…but you're going to go home, and one day it will just…just hit you… and then you'll know." Even in the darkness his eyes consumed her. She held her breath as she absorbed the features of his face. He was the only thing that existed in that moment. She audibly exhaled and rested her head on his shoulder. She could feel her heart pulsing against her chest. He rested his head on hers and stared into the night. She knew what she needed to do, but had no idea how she would get there.

***

"Three more sets of push-ups then we will switch to burpies!"

"You've got to be kidding me," Cassandra bemoaned. *Push-ups? Burpies?* Those were all of the things she got smoked with at Basic Training. She didn't need the work-out. Just the warm-up was kicking her butt.

Cassandra flipped over on the mat into a puddle of her own sweat. "That ends this HIIT round. Time to bring the heart rate down."

"Oh thank God," Cassandra breathed. Maybe now that the workout was starting she could finally catch her breath.

She fixed her gaze on the black and red emblem resting at eye level. She imagined it to represent the head of her problem. Her eyes narrowed. She knew exactly what to do. Jab, cross. Left hook, uppercut. Right roundhouse, left front kick. Jab cross, jab cross. Cassandra wrestled her bag back to its starting position before continuing to voice her concerns and complaints. In her moments of frustrations, she always joked about wanting to punch people in the face. She never knew how satisfying punching something could actually be, although she had her suspicions. She felt alive and invigorated. She twisted and turned rhythmically to the music and imagined her frustrations melting away with every punch.

Every kick was a confirmation that she intended to fight back and not take anyone's crap anymore. His lies. His allegations. His hurtful words. His attempts to draw her out. His very presence. He wouldn't get to her anymore, at least not today, and at least not for a few more hours until the endorphins wore off. She was a new woman. She may need to remind herself of this tomorrow, but for today, she believed every word of it.

Cassandra jumped into her truck and headed to her next challenge. This would be the first day in the office since Brandon left. She didn't realize the full weight of his departure until she walked into the building. She entered not expecting to see him, and received every bit of what she was anticipating. Of course she knew he was gone, but somehow she thought she needed to do her due diligence and look. Maybe she had overlooked something and he didn't deploy after all. Maybe he was in his office waiting for her to stop by and ask him about his day. Maybe he was sent home from the mobilization site due to some unforeseen medical or personnel issue. Maybe he would be waiting for her if she just looked hard enough. Maybe.

As her search for Brandon came up empty handed, Cassandra paused beneath his picture in the hallway. He was important people. Important enough to have his picture up on the wall. If he couldn't be there physically, at least a piece of him still remained.

In truth, Cassandra didn't have to look far to see evidence of his presence. The armory was full of pieces of him. His staff all bore remnants of his personality. His policies, his procedures, his very command had the essence of Brandon Fletcher stamped all over them. The motor pool was an act of his creation. The way he organized and stored his equipment. The way his personnel were trained to react quickly and succinctly to every situation. Cassandra smiled knowing Brandon was never really far away. He was as close as her heart and mind allowed him to be.

What didn't make Cassandra smile was David and his latest attempt at co-parenting. She recoiled every time she received a text message from him. She wondered if anyone had ever claimed PTSD from a cell phone jingle. If she thought she could live without her phone, she would. She strained to see the message through clenched hands. But she didn't need to see it again, she already knew what it said. She already knew she wanted to kill him. Every time she felt like she was getting her life back together, David would show up and remind her why she went to counseling in the first place.

Cassandra grabbed the travel size devotional from her desk and turned to the verse of the day. Forgiveness. It wasn't doing it for her. She grabbed her work phone to reach out to Brandon. She didn't want to be a training distraction. She opened her email to distract herself with the day's inquiries but other people's problems did nothing for her. She cried out, "I don't know what you're trying to do, but you can knock it off. Whatever you are trying to teach me isn't working. I'm done!" Cassandra didn't know if her words had any impact on her spiritual well-being, but they were honest. She really couldn't do this anymore. She didn't know if she could stand up to David, but she knew at least God would let her talk.

God was often a topic of conversation between her and Brandon. Although Brandon considered Cassandra to be true to her faith, the reality was she struggled to hold on every single day. If anyone ever wondered how many surgeries a spouse with small children could take before they snapped, the answer was four. Brandon recognized her hardships through an unfiltered religious lens, often acting with more grace and poise than those who claimed the official affiliation. He often struggled with the finer points of Christianity, yet could easily discern moments he felt God's hand in his life. Cassandra didn't pretend to be attuned to God's will in her own life, but couldn't help but think Brandon entered her life on purpose. It was just for *what* purpose she struggled to ascertain. As much as she cared for him, she often wondered what God was trying to prove by keeping Brandon just out of reach.

***

Cassandra snuggled up in bed with the covers tucked under her chin. His voice echoed like a warm melody in her ear. He was her favorite bedtime story. The phone didn't do him justice, but would have to suffice for tonight. Cassandra wished she could have spoken with him under better circumstances. As it was, she had to pick and choose her moments. Although she had been waiting for months for her divorce to finalize, not everyone in the household exercised the same level of patience.

"…I'm just not sure what I'm going to do Brandon..." Cassandra's words stopped mid-sentence as David came up the stairs. Maybe if she pretended she was sleeping he would leave her alone.

"Who are you talking to?" he questioned as he walked into the bedroom. Cassandra held her breath. She would take the punishment, but he would leave Brandon out of this.

"I'm talking to my friends," she stated as nonchalantly as she could muster.

"You're talking to *him* aren't you?!" David demanded.

Cassandra prepped for the storm that was inevitably coming and restated, "I'm talking to my friends."

"You're talking to him, I knew it…" David's string of accusations trailed off as he left the bedroom.

"Are you still there?" Cassandra breathed, in a barely audible tone.

"Yes, I'm still here," Brandon reassured her.

"He was just in here demanding to know who I was talking to and…" Before she could finish her thought the bedroom door flew open and David reentered. He headed towards the closet talking nonsensically as he threw objects on the bed. Cassandra asked him to leave.

David scoffed, "You want me to leave?! This is my house too. I'm not going anywhere," he stated as he made his way over to the bathroom. The slough of hygienic items parading from the medicine cabinet apparently needed immediate claiming. "This is mine…this is mine…oh what's this? Wax? You'll shave for him and not for me?!" He reached for the tiny wicker box underneath the bed. "I better take these too before you get any ideas. I should count them first to make sure none of them were used." David stormed down the hallway with his assortment of prizes in hand.

Cassandra felt paralyzed with fear and shame. She was embarrassed Brandon had to hear that. She shuttered through freshly formed tears, "Are you still there?" She looked down at her phone and wondered the exact minute he had hung up. Knowing David's emotional energy was spent for the evening, Cassandra reached back out. She couldn't have an evening like that and not hear from him.

She confessed the horror she felt at David's accusations. "You just have to get through it. It will all be over soon," he offered.

"How can I Brandon? How can I move on when he won't let me?" She paused as her heart sank. "How can we even be friends when he won't let us?"

Brandon's reassuring temperament slipped away and all he could offer Cassandra in that moment was a broken "I…I don't know…I don't…" Cassandra bowed her head. "Look, why don't you just… just call me in the morning…and we can…we can chat then." David had won the battle and Cassandra hung up the phone. It wasn't supposed to end like this. She had to make it right.

In the moments that passed between her text inquiry and her next phone call, Brandon's reassurance returned in full force. He was armed with constructive platitudes and helpful insight into Cassandra's situation. David would never get over it, and she would. He was just lashing out. She just had to get through this. Not sure if she believed him or not, Cassandra appreciated his sentiment and efforts to bring her peace. David surmised that Brandon had been the reason for her divorce. In Cassandra's eyes, Brandon was the only thing getting her through it.

She clung to him in the weeks and months to follow. Those first few months were the worst. A self imposed contact ban was placed on them by both parties at various times. Brandon wanted to give her space to work through her emotions without the added stress of trying to justify their friendship, and Cassandra wanted to give Brandon space to recharge and not be pulled into the middle of her failing relationship. Contact consisted mainly of text messages and scheduled phone calls. Drill weekends and staff meetings also afforded the opportunity for them to touch base without the added complexity of unstable onlookers. Neither one of them seemed pleased with the arrangement, Cassandra just happened to be more vocal about it.

It was drill weekend, a cherished time for Cassandra. It was like her reward for making it through another season of *As Cassandra's World Turns*. Drama or not, Brandon recharged her battery and was one of her closest friends. He was standing right in front of her, yet she missed him terribly. "I have a proposition for you," she began.

Reading her body language and tone of voice, her lieutenant gestured his chin over his shoulder and responded, "I'm just going to go down the hall to get something. I'll be back in a bit."

The little school girl in her blushed as Brandon's cool blue eyes fixated on hers. He crossed his arms. This was serious business. Cassandra breathed before finding her voice. "I know we're not really supposed to be hanging out these days, but I was wondering…if you would consider lifting the travel ban this weekend… for Veteran's Day."

He leaned intently into his crossed arms. He looked serious. Maybe she had made a mistake asking and turned her attention towards an unkempt stack of papers. "Well," Brandon began finally, "the tattoo expo is this weekend…"

Not sure if he had heard her request, Cassandra eased, "Okaaaaay…"

With arms still crossed, Brandon leaned forward as if to tell her a secret. "You could go with me."

"Oh." Not exactly what she had in mind. "When is it?"

"Saturday."

"I was thinking maybe about going out to lunch," Cassandra suggested.

"There's a football game this weekend too," Brandon offered. A football game…that's how it all began… "It's on Sunday at 10."

10 o'clock was church time. Perhaps Cassandra could convince little people they would rather attend the early morning service. Perhaps she could also convince other people they would enjoy watching her kids too.

Being a veteran, it seemed almost contradictory Cassandra never took much interest in the holiday prior to that day. Veteran's Day usually meant free food, a day off of work, and various forms of well wishes from countless passersby. Today it meant something entirely different, and she could hardly contain herself at the possibilities that awaited. Cassandra never had great luck at the *Sports Page*, but maybe God would smile on her and throw her a bone. It was at that very establishment her life began to unravel just a few short months ago. Either the place was jinxed, or she was just bad luck for football and all those who chose to partake.

Cassandra's eyes adjusted to the dim lighting as she scanned the room for a familiar face. Her eyes were drawn to the back corner where Brandon sat watching his team kick off. She paused before proceeding, wondering why he had chosen such a large table. "Are you expecting a lot of people?"

Brandon's eyes found hers as she approached. "Just you." Cassandra reached for the seat across from him when he chimed in, "Not sure if you'll be able to see the game from there, you can slide over here if you want," motioning to the seat next to his. Cassandra's smile widened. Maybe today would be different after all.

His eyes were on the game but were also on her. He alternated game time wisdom and rivalry background with post deployment plans and witty anecdotes. He asked her how she was doing and what her plans for the rest of the weekend were. The months of deprivation began to slip away as she allowed Brandon to fill her heart with his presence. It was like they had never been apart. As Brandon spoke, Cassandra felt like she was seeing him for the first time; beautiful, thought provoking and suddenly available. She couldn't believe she was sitting next to someone so amazing. The way Brandon looked at her made her think that maybe she was pretty amazing too.

Cassandra pretended not to look him over as he walked away to use the restroom. His un-tucked shirt conformed completely to the curves of this body. His jeans left just enough to the imagination to leave you guessing on preferred underwear type and style. She pretended not to do the same as he made his way back to the table. He reached for his unanswered cell phone as it vied for his attention. He scanned the message before throwing it on the table and turning away. He picked it up and pushed it towards Cassandra as a familiar name scrolled across the locked screen. She was hesitant to ask him to unlock it so she could see the rest of the message. She was fairly certain she already knew what it said.

Brandon leaned over her shoulder as she read the words out loud. "*…everything was fine until you came along…I know you two are together…next time pick someone else's wife to hang out with…*" Brandon's anger flared through his nostrils as Cassandra instinctively reached for her phone. Similar sentiment populated on her screen, except she would get an added reminder of being engaged six years ago on this date. He blamed her for his own mental instability. He blamed her for not knowing that today was hard for him. He blamed her for filing for divorce.

Cassandra placed a hand on Brandon's shoulder. He recoiled at her touch as she let the anger pass through her. She knew he wasn't mad at her, David was a lot for anyone to take. If she knew filing for divorce would have created such widespread venom, she would have just silently suffered. Cassandra was not looking forward to David being there when she got home. She didn't know how she would deal with him, but she couldn't think about that now and had to focus on the moment. She had to focus on Brandon.

Brandon's hands shook as he handled his phone, reliving David's anger. "For your own mental well-being, you need to block his number," Cassandra stated.

"I don't know how. I would click on his number, but I'm afraid of it calling him." Fear. That was a new emotion for Brandon.

Cassandra experimented on her own phone with an emotionally unattached number. "Here, just do this," she instructed as she turned her screen towards him. Brandon leaned over her shoulder and followed her actions. He tossed the phone on the table and searched her face.

"I don't hate a lot of people, but I want to stab him in the face." The seriousness of his expression made Cassandra chuckle. She often felt the same way.

The very first time she came to the *Sports Page* it was filled with much the same drama. Their month long training event had finally ended. The convoy home was excruciating in the summer sun, and with each passing mile her desire to not return home consumed her. She missed the kids and wanted to see them, but just not anyone else that lived in the house. By the time she made it to her front door, she scarcely had the energy to make it up the stairs. She was home. Everyone was happy she was there, except her.

In the days that followed, Cassandra sank deeper into her unhappiness until David finally commented on her mood. She couldn't hold it back anymore, she had to tell him. Cassandra's heart ached at his pain, but she was also aware of her own pain that existed long before that day. All she wanted was for him to try. She had made the request for the entirety of their marriage with limited effort and buy in. Cassandra's heart broke a little each day, and it wasn't until the final surgery that she realized just how many pieces she actually held in her hand.

That week Cassandra met Brandon for lunch. It was in that moment she realized just how genuine their connection really was. He put his arm around her in a quiet moment in his kitchen and pulled her in close for an embrace. His eyes grew soft and he asked her if she wanted to watch a football game with him that weekend. She agreed and had a babysitter come out to watch the kids. That night, David went through her phone, harassing the people that allowed the outing to happen. From that moment, harassing Brandon became David's number one pastime.

Cassandra turned towards Brandon and surveyed his face. She hoped David's text didn't ruin his day. She could see his shoulders start to relax. His breath steadied and a grin began to pull at the edges of his mouth. He gazed at her in quiet appreciation. Even in his anger he never stopped seeing her. She was always right in front of him. Cassandra didn't know if she could ever get used to being seen.

He pulled the check towards him. Even after all that he was still offering to buy her lunch. The rain began to pour as he walked her to the truck. He pulled her in close, and was in no hurry to escape the downpour. "Thanks for coming out, I had fun." Despite everything, Cassandra had too. She felt her heart thumping in his embrace. The only thing he was holding against her was himself. Who was this man, she wondered? Someone unlike anyone she had ever met. For better or for worse, Cassandra knew she needed him in her life, even if that meant having to pay a tax.

***

Cassandra paced in the lobby as she stared out the large bay window. It wasn't long before she saw a familiar white truck drive through the parking lot. She waved wildly to get his attention before realizing the odds of him seeing her through the tinted restaurant windows were slim. She pretended to hide her excitement as he rounded the corner and entered the door. Her smile widened as he approached, until her ear to ear grin erupted into a wild embrace. He did his best to pass it off as a one armed greeting, but Cassandra knew better. She could tell he was excited to see her too.

Lunch was nice. He noticed her wool coat and did his best to suppress an impish grin as he sat across from her. It was finally over, and she could at last tell him the final installment. Although the decision threatened to financially devastate her, at least now she had a chance to obtain the life she wanted. Cassandra grinned as she traced the outline of his face. A big part of the life she wanted was sitting right in front of her.

Brandon listened with a tender sincerity as she spoke. It had been Cassandra's story, but really it was Brandon's too. The text message harassments, the emergency mental health phone calls, her attempts to move on with her life; he was nearly as invested as she was. His eyes, his voice, even the sharp edges of his face seemed softer as Cassandra regaled her final marital encounter. The air between them was mounting with an eager anticipation. Cassandra was at last legally permitted to look, and she took it all in.

A sheepish grin sat on Brandon's face almost the entirety of their conversation. There was a park nearby she often took the kids to in the hopes of "accidently" running into him since it was near his home. She offered it to him now, and despite the brisk February air, he agreed.

They walked side by side through the park's paths before deciding to make their own. Cassandra wondered what the odds were of holding his hand. Seeing them buried deep in his jean pockets, she determined not likely. As they walked, she slid her arm through his and gave a gentle squeeze. He continued in conversation, and proceeded to offer his usual world view commentary. He stopped a few times to send her an affectionate gaze as they recounted familiar similarities, like her birthday. It was the same day as his sister's.

They often shared the same views of work, relationships and life in general. They agreed on most things, except for where they wanted to achieve them. Cassandra wanted to stay on the West Coast. Brandon wanted to move back to the Midwest with his family. Cassandra sighed. They were so close yet so far away. Not wanting to be the thing that stood in the way of his own happiness, Cassandra offered, "I'll miss you when you go," as she rested her head on his chest.

He wrapped his arms around her and rested his head on hers stating, “I’ll miss you too,” as he paused to admire her choice of shampoo. Despite the apparent chill, the conversation continued long into the afternoon.

At one point he pulled back to study the curves of her face as he stated, “The Army doesn’t deserve me,” before adding a bold, “They don’t deserve you either.” Cassandra believed it was a matter of perspective, but he had a way of making everything sound convincing. She squeezed his arm and tilted her gaze towards his.

Brandon shuttered in one last attempt to shield himself from the crisp winter breeze. “We should get going.”

They paused in the parking lot to absorb the last bit of afternoon sunshine. Goodbyes were both Cassandra’s favorite time and least favorite time of the outing. Favorite because goodbyes meant hugs. Least favorite because hugs meant farewell. Maybe things would end differently this time.

Brandon must have been thinking the same thing when he gave a “Now we’re the same height” observation as Cassandra hopped up on the curb. He had a softness to his eyes and a gentleness to his tone that she couldn’t help but notice. She wondered if this could be the moment.

She wrapped her arms around him and whispered, “I want to kiss you.”

Brandon paused as he contorted his lips into a cautiously skeptic gesture, before responding, “I don’t kiss.”

Cassandra's confusion was only temporary as she pulled him in for a staggered embrace. Their faces sat side by side and she could feel Brandon's heart beating on top of hers. It was beating fast and his breath quickened. If kissing was something he really didn't do, she imagined his anxiety level rising with each passing moment.

She rested her forehead against his as she broke the embrace. His breaths continued to multiply as she brushed her cheek against the roughness of his. Cassandra pulled back just long enough to run her fingers along the edges of his face before pressing her lips against his. She was firm but gentle. She was quick. Brandon stood still, seemingly dazed by what had just happened. As Cassandra began to pull away, it was as if an imaginary force field was broken, and Brandon moved towards her to offer an innocent peck. He missed her lips. She tried again. It was as if his kissing bone had been activated, and he was responding with a delayed reaction. Cassandra stared at Brandon quizzically and moved in one final time. Brandon's lips stayed pressed to hers. She wondered if maybe there was some truth in his statement.

Just as quickly as the kiss had filled her with anxious anticipation, its parting filled her with embarrassment and regret. Perhaps sensing her uneasiness, Brandon offered her an extended embrace. She stood in his arms as shame washed over her. "Come on you," he uttered softly. "We should go."

The three minute drive back to his truck was excruciating. Maybe she should have waited to kiss him until more than three days after her divorce.

Cassandra pretended to concentrate on the traffic in the roundabout. Brandon laughed from the passenger seat. "You're crazy," he chuckled.

Alarmed, Cassandra asked, "*Why*?"

"For wanting to kiss me a guy like me," he stated as he shot a grin her direction.

Embarrassment pulled on her heartstrings as she answered, "You have a lot to offer. I think you sell yourself short." Maybe it was Cassandra that was selling herself short by thinking he hadn't enjoyed the experience. In the safety of the restaurant parking lot Brandon offered another hug. Despite her embarrassment, Cassandra wanted another kiss.

"A little at a time," Brandon cautioned. "Look, I'm just now at the point where hugging isn't the worst thing in the world. Maybe next time we can see a movie." Cassandra's heart leapt. Movies meant he would consider kissing her again, scientific fact.

Cassandra gazed at their reflection in the side of her truck door, watching as an ear to ear smile erupted across his face. Maybe she hadn't ruined things after all. He looked content, the most content she had ever seen him. Brandon caught a glimpse of his smile and quickly abandoned it before focusing his attention on her. "This is the happiest I've seen *you* in a while." Not accepting that *he* could be the reason for her happiness, he concluded, "I just think you're glad that the stress of the divorce is done." Probably true. Him giving her a reason to smile, probably also true.

As he walked back to his truck, Brandon paused to make deliberate eye contact with her. He held her gaze as he offered her his signature *Captain of the*

Football Team smile stating, “I had fun. Thanks for coming out.” His eye contact devoured her. Her inner teenage girl swooned as she watched the hottest guy on the football team walk away.

***

Cassandra stared at her computer. Not even sure what she was supposed to be looking at, she scrolled aimlessly from webpage to webpage hoping something would ring a bell. Evaluations. New physical fitness standards. Maintenance inspections. Logistical resources. It all mattered, but to Cassandra had become white noise. She had so many things she wanted to accomplish, but with Brandon gone, she wasn’t sure where to even place her focus. Maybe he *had* occupied most of her conscious energy. Maybe it was a good thing that he left. Maybe now she could focus on herself, free of distraction. Her thoughts were taken away to the curve of his smile and the warmth of his arms. If only he knew how difficult he was making this.

He had been gone for two weeks and the first Brandon-less drill was less than a week away. In the post deployment apocalypse, her support section was reduced by half, their units had lost significant logistical capability and an all new leadership regime had emerged. The second wave of the deployment outbreak left the staff fragmented, under resourced and pulled in multiple directions. Cassandra often wondered what the point of it all was. She didn’t have the energy to start over, not again. Her life had been nothing but restarts since she signed the final paperwork in February. There was nothing stable left for her to hold onto. Other people might have welcomed the opportunity for change, but Cassandra lost the available resources to cope. With more changes threatening on the horizon, she headed towards drill with unrelenting dread.

With two thirds of the brigade deployed or on their way out, there were very few units left to support. Cassandra thought of the new incoming Executive Officer and wondered if she would be relegated to being a glorified secretary to her same rank counterpart. Recruiting and retention were the new number one priority; maybe she would just smile and tell people everything would be okay if they joined the National Guard. Her Soldiers skill sets would undoubtedly regress if they had no one to support. Everything Cassandra created would be undone. Brandon had been there to hold her hand through the first apocalyptic wave, who would hold her hand until he returned? She pushed the intrusive thoughts from her head. She had to conserve her energy if she had any hope of making it till Friday.

Then drill, as it often did, had a way of taking on an energy all its own. As the eleventh hour approached, Cassandra found herself invigorated by all of the changes and sought to take control of her section and direction for the fiscal year. She drafted counseling statements, refined her timeline, and took their logistical shortfall and turned it into a teachable moment. This year would be challenging, and her staff could be part of the solution. She would provide them the leadership they had not been afforded during the rush of deployment planning.

Drill rolled through like a freight train right through October and into November. With less than two weeks between the events, Cassandra could scarcely recall any defining events that separated the two. The distraction of mandatory briefs, classes and new leadership philosophies consumed most of her time and attention. Physical fitness testing and officer mentorship occupied the rest. She thought back to her previous round of officers prior to the onset of the apocalypse. They were the best. Training new officers was tiring and often frustrating. She longed for familiar faces and wondered how their deployment experience was treating them thus far.

They weren't the only ones that were missed. Although Cassandra knew not to expect Brandon for the weekend's festivities, she couldn't help but look for him everywhere she went. She scanned the briefings for his face. She panned the formation for signs of him. She peered across the room expecting to see him seated at the command and staff meeting. She wondered if she would catch him roaming the hallways. If she sat in her office long enough, maybe he would stop by to say hi. She knew her experience without him wasn't the same. She wondered how his experience was without her. A simple "I miss you," was often returned with "I miss working together." He missed at least a part of her.

Drill left Cassandra feeling mentally and emotionally exhausted. It was a lot of work to invest in something you weren't quite sure you believed in. She wrote four operations orders in three days and had drill hangover. Mondays were the worst, especially this one. Operations hangover plus physical fitness hangover rendered her almost immobile the rest of the week. Luckily for her most of the staff was at a conference on the coast and expected little of her. Once her first few mandatory tasks were complete, her desire to complete anything else was virtually nonexistent. She needed something else to focus on. She needed a break.

November was National Novel Writing Month, a task she had every intention of participating in until drill sidelined her efforts. Although symptoms of the hangover still persisted, she knew if she didn't take action now she would miss her chance. In college Cassandra majored in English Writing. Even now, she had as much ability to be creative as she did back then; next to none. Creativity always seemed to elude her, and she simply didn't know how to make up a world of characters and personalities and events that seemed believable. Every attempt she made felt forced and superficial. Maybe she should stick with what she knew.

But Cassandra often wondered what *did* she know? She knew she had two small children and an ex-husband who was intent on criticizing her every action, both as a mother and as a human being. She knew she was tired and depleted, and needed all the help she could get to make it through this next year without her biggest supporter. She knew at times she was difficult to get along with and often struggled to find purpose. Maybe this exercise would give her the purpose she needed to dig a little deeper. Cassandra recalled the last few years. Where would she even start? Brandon. He was really the heart of it. Maybe she would start there.

***

"Are we still on for drinks after work today?" she asked as Brandon shuffled from one pile of paper to the next.

"Yes... I just might need a little more time to finish up," he stated as he reached for his next stack of priorities. "Give me another half hour, I'll meet you there," he affirmed as he flashed his signature grin.

It was nice having him in the same building that she worked. Ever since the mobilization went public, federal dollars abounded left and right to support mission requirements. Cassandra wasn't entirely sure what the mission was exactly, but she was convinced Brandon was the right person for the job. She gave his name to her Battalion Commander for consideration, and although her request was initially met with resistance by both parties, they soon put aside their differences and made it official. The last two weeks had been nice. With another six months to go, Cassandra was sure she could get her Brandon fill before he went out the door.

Between him wrapping up his duties with the Army Corp of Engineers and both of them changing residencies, almost a month passed since they kissed. Tonight was the first time she would see him outside of work since that fateful afternoon. As the hours ticked away, her anticipation began to grow. She wasn't sure if Brandon considered this to be a date, but it was starting to feel like one to her. Cassandra questioned whether the evening would move their relationship forward, or if it would end in awkward defeat. She had to focus. This wouldn't be different than any of the other times they had hung out.

A tingly sensation began to course through Cassandra's body as she sat poised at the brew pub table. The sides of her neck started to tense. She inhaled deeply and steadied her breath. Her eyes were drawn to the barroom doors as they flew open, and followed Brandon to the table where he launched his keys. He plopped down in his chair without saying a word. He looked tired and did not look pleased. Grumpy Brandon was here, and he was not her favorite. Her plans for a relaxing evening began to slowly slip away.

Cassandra wished he would have let her buy him that drink before he arrived, at least he'd have something to take the edge off. She wasn't quite sure where his source of anger was coming from, but she knew she needed to find out if she had any hopes of having a decent evening. "What's wrong?" she asked. Brandon rolled his eyes. *Everything*. His impending deadlines, other people's incompetence, time management. More appropriately, Cassandra should have asked if anything *wasn't* wrong. She sighed. This was going to be a long evening.

Brandon hit the beer early and often, and after the first two, started to slip off his angry exterior and settled into a more approachable version of himself. Encouraged by his emotional shift, Cassandra took it as an invitation to move from her seat across the table to the one next to his. Brandon hunched his shoulders and looked away. His awkward posture recovered and turned towards her. "I have a bone to pick with you," he stated as his eyes locked hers. They were intense.

Had she done something wrong? Maybe he was just overreacting. Cassandra searched his face for any available indications. It was a toss-up.

"I was late today because I ran into Sergeant Thompson on my way out," Brandon began. "He wanted to get some signatures from me on some pay documents." The plot seemed pretty straight forward so far and Cassandra nodded for him to continue. "I told him I had to get going because I was late to meet you. He smirked at me and replied 'Oooh, you mean like a date?'" Cassandra could see where this was going, suddenly the punch line was in sight. He continued, "I asked him what he was talking about. He hesitated before he told me about *Red Robin…*" Cassandra lowered her head. "I asked him where he had heard about that… he said he heard it from you." His gaze pinned her against the barroom wall.

Cassandra sat guilty as charged and would take her punishment. "Is that why you were angry when you got here?" she ventured.

Brandon nodded his head. The intensity in his eyes continued. "Why are you talking to my Readiness NCO about that? My personal life is nobody's business." Cassandra felt convicted. She didn't know why she had talked to him or anyone else about Brandon. Maybe she felt comfortable and thought she could trust others with her secrets. Apparently her Sergeant Thompson meter was off.

The intensity in his eyes softened as he continued out her sentence. "Look, back when I was enlisted, I had a little too much to drink and wound up kissing Sara Thomas. One person saw and told everybody. I don't want people knowing my personal life. It's none of their business."

"But you didn't do anything wrong," Cassandra interjected.

"That's not the point," Brandon reasoned. "It's the perception. You *just* got divorced…we work together…I don't want people spreading rumors." Cassandra lowered her head. She wondered if he was ashamed at the thought of being together. "No more talking to people about my personal life, okay?" She nodded as he gave her arm a squeeze. "Well, I feel better," he affirmed as he gulped the last of his beer. Cassandra was so confused. All she knew was that she didn't like the idea of Brandon being mad at her, even if only temporarily.

But with each smile and glance into the depths of his eyes, Cassandra's shame began to disappear. His presence was intoxicating. He was like a power cord that charged her depleted battery. She tested the waters by brushing her shoulder against his as he spoke. She saw his hand resting on the table and wondered if he would notice if she slipped hers underneath. She felt it tense as he uttered an audible sigh. Holding hands didn't really seem like his thing.

Brandon carried on, albeit somewhat distracted, as he wrapped up his current conversation. Transitioning to the next topic, he pumped her hand as if tossing an object away. Thinking her hand had somehow slipped from his, Cassandra reached over to reinitiate contact. Brandon's sigh was more pronounced than the first, as he cited, "You and your hand holding…We can hold hands, but we're going to be friends." Cassandra tuned out the last part. All she heard was that he would hold her hand.

Brandon's tone audibly shifted and soon lost its rough edges. They talked about relationships, Army experiences and general life. His hand enveloped hers. He stroked it gently before giving it a discernible squeeze. Cassandra took that as permission to squeeze back. Brandon inhaled sharply as he coughed out his freshly poured beer and excused himself to the restroom. Maybe he wasn't ready for that level of hand holding.

As he returned, he gingerly set himself down in the chair next to hers and glanced at her with a nervous energy that was new. Cassandra wasn't sure what to make of his expression, and leaned in to kiss him before she lost her nerve. He turned his head at the final moment before exclaiming, "No. We're friends." Wide eyed, Cassandra lowered herself back into her chair.

Another sigh escaped Brandon's mouth as he offered, "Look, I'm a great friend. You need something, I am there, but there are different levels of relationships. There's acquaintance, friend, best friend...I can only go so far in my relationships…I can't go past a certain point." Cassandra stared at him in disbelief. He was ending their relationship before it even had a chance to begin. "As a friend…you *love* me…" The words hung in his mouth like a foreign phrase. "You would not like me in an intimate relationship." He omitted another sigh. "I don't want to hurt you."

She didn't understand. Why would he go through the motions of kissing her and holding her hand if he didn't want to be with her? Unable to contain her thoughts, Cassandra burst out, "Then why did you let me kiss you?!"

Brandon's shoulders sank with the same level of sorrow Cassandra had experienced earlier in the evening. The brightness in his eyes turned to shame as he uttered, "Because I didn't want to hurt you." It was back to that. He didn't want to hurt her, yet in that moment was doing the very thing he claimed he would never do. The sadness behind his eyes did little to appease her emotions. Brandon continued to complicate matters by offering further sentiment. "I don't want you to think that I don't care about you, because that's not true." He reached his arm around her shoulder and pulled her in. Cassandra turned to face him and nestled her nose into his cheek. Brandon assured, "I wouldn't be hanging out with you if I didn't like you." He searched her face with a tender sincerity. He hoped she knew he meant it.

As she stared into his eyes, Cassandra saw her past, present and future all at once. The lunches…the dinners…the drinks…the football games…the movie they would never see…the way he played with her children…the way he endured untold harassment just to assure her everything would be okay. This wasn't how it was supposed to end. She had so much more to the story, and couldn't believe this chapter was coming to a close.

It was raining again. He popped his hood up as he walked her to her truck. She thanked him for the evening and for having been her friend. Alarmed, Brandon responded, "We still *are* friends," and wrapped his arms tightly around her. Cassandra's heart quickened in his embrace as it always had, only this time she wasn't supposed to feel it. She would never understand men. They were so complicated. Maybe she would just add love to the list of things she was no good at.

Having slept on her somber evening, Cassandra awoke refreshed and newly invigorated. She hadn't realized just how much energy her obsession with Brandon really had taken up. So little energy had been left for anything else. Not sure how to expend her newfound fortune, she ventured to work fully aware of her surroundings and everyone around her. Somehow the weekly meeting seemed less boring, others quirks didn't irritate her as much, and even her supervisor's demands seemed less harsh. Then there was Brandon. Cassandra wasn't sure what she was supposed to feel around him, or what she was still even allowed to feel. He said they were friends. She pressed through the embarrassment of a "Good morning" greeting and continued on her way. He asked to speak with her about the logistical support for pre-mobilization training. He was back. Everything would be okay.

The energy continued as she made her way to daycare to pick up the kids. The incessant questioning from the back seat intermixed with the inevitable whining that ensued only rated at mild irritation. Maybe there was nothing wrong with being friends. He was a great friend, Brandon said so himself. Maybe she needed to stop focusing on friendship as a consolation prize, but instead as *the* prize. She would be the best friend she could be.

It wasn't long before Brandon agreed to get drinks again. This time, he would invite her to his apartment. Not on purpose, it just seemed like the logical solution to an already overbooked conference call schedule. They could meet up at 5:00 PM. They would have one hour.

Cassandra beat him there and pulled up a stool on the first floor of his apartment building. A built in bar, how clever she observed. She saw Brandon standing in the doorway and pretended she didn't notice. She continued to not notice as he ordered a drink and made his way over to the table. She didn't notice him pulling a stool close to hers at the oversized table, or the impish grin that spread across his face as he settled in. She didn't notice him leaning inside her bubble to show her pictures on his cell phone. She noticed none of it.

What Cassandra did notice was him checking the time. "We have about ten minutes until my call," Brandon warned. Ten minutes was just the right amount of time.

Cassandra tied up their work related conversation and moved into the next phase of her plan. "Do you have time for a quick tour?"

He repeated her words before adding, "Yeah. Let's go."

Brandon's apartment complex had a very motel type feel. Cassandra wondered if the building had ever been converted. She followed him into the elevator, pretending to not notice the feeling of excitement bubbling in her stomach. She was about to see his apartment. He had just moved in and she imagined not many others could claim to have visited. But it didn't matter, they were just friends.

As they crossed the threshold into Brandon's personal living space, Cassandra was struck by the size of it. The room was scarcely bigger than her living room, except this one boasted a kitchen and "bedroom" space within its walls. The laundry and the bathroom were conveniently co-located in the adjoining room, and the cabinets and storage areas were tucked out of sight to conserve precious floor space. His apartment was sparsely populated much like his house had been. A single desk chair and table sat in the "living room," and a black Army tough box supported his television. His bed stood prominently between the bathroom and hallway entrance.

Not sure where to focus her energies, Cassandra made her way to the kitchen area and surmised, "Wow. Everything is...right there." The miniature kitchen boasted all of the normal items one might expect to find ordinarily; a toaster oven, pots, pans and dishes. Her eyes were drawn to a small pile of books resting on the counter. There were three. She picked them up one by one and silently read the titles. *Venus and Mars Starting Over; His Needs, Her Needs; Enneagram Personality Traits.* Surprised that such subjects would be associated with cooking, Cassandra inquired, "Are these *yours*?" Brandon lowered his head, uttering something about a friend suggesting them. He took the enneagram book from her hands and began to give his synopsis.

"For years I thought I was a Six," he asserted. "After re-taking the test, it turns out I'm a One. Read that and see if that doesn't sound like me," he stated as he thrust his cell phone into her hand. *The Perfectionist: High moral character, severe inner critic, anger caused by unmet needs, afraid to make a mistake.* Yep. That sounded just like him. "Do you know what that means?!" Cassandra shook her head and waited for the punch line. "It means I've been working on the wrong things this whole time!"

The screen on his cell phone flickered, reminding her of Brandon's conference call deadline. "What time is it?" she inquired.

"It's almost six." It was time for his call. She wasn't ready to go, and suggested they continue their conversation. Brandon agreed and offered, "How about Monday over lunch?" That seemed a little too far away for Cassandra.

"How long is your conference call?" she asked.

"About thirty minutes."

Cassandra formulated her thoughts. She would need to proceed with caution. "How about I hang out for thirty minutes and we can continue this discussion after you're done?"

Brandon shifted his weight from one foot to another. His discomfort was evident. He started, "The call could go longer than that," before transitioning into, "I'm not sure if I'll be in the mood to hang out." He tried again. "I'm expecting someone over later," before deciding on, "It's up to you."

Cassandra surveyed his face. No doubt having her is his apartment came with certain ramifications, friendship or not. "How about I hang out for thirty minutes, and if you're not in the mood to hang out or it runs long, I can always go." Relieved, Brandon nodded in agreement and dialed his number.

Not wanting to stake claim to his bed, Cassandra sat on the floor in front of it and scrolled through her Facebook feed. There was nothing of relative importance, it just a way to distract herself from the fact that she was in the hottest-guy-on-the-football-team's apartment. But she kept forgetting; they were just friends.

True to his word, the call lasted twenty-eight minutes. Still taking calls afterwards, he walked passed Cassandra to use the restroom. He closed the door but left it open just enough for her to notice. She planted her gaze in the middle of Tommy's latest trip to Florida, and Angela's marathon run in DC. They were friends, she wasn't allowed to look.

Her eyes were still tuned into the Florida excursion when she felt a tap on her leg. Startled, she looked up to find Brandon crouched at eye level. "Ready for that drink?"

Her heart leapt with excitement before she decided on a more conservative answer of, "Sure." She closed the chapter on Florida vacations and followed him downstairs, ready to reengage with her favorite logistician.

The tavern was now dimly lit, and Brandon escorted her to the bar to place their order. She slid her money on the counter and he slid it back to her. This one was on him. He offered a chair at a nearby table, and slowly slunk down across from her. His face was soft in the glow of the candlelight. His eyes were bright as a warm smile stretched across his face. This night was perfect, and was how Cassandra envisioned their previous encounter going.

For the next hour and a half they discussed the Army, life and relationship realizations. This time Cassandra *did* notice his face soften, and the emergence of his Brandon Fletcher signature look of infatuation. She wondered if there was any room for infatuation in friendship. Whoever he was supposed to meet never materialized, or Brandon had simply told them not to come. Either way, she was glad he chose to spend time with her as his first option.

Brandon's infatuation eventually gave way to fatigue and started to yawn. "Sorry I'm so tired. Maybe we should call it a night." They toasted one last drink and Brandon walked her to her truck. He gave her an extended embrace as the warmth of his touch washed over her. "Thanks for coming out to where I live, I had fun. Have a good night Cassandra." First names were rarely used. Cassandra blamed it on the military culture. As she walked away, she glanced over her shoulder to find him doing the same. He lingered as she climbed into her truck, offering a familiar wave as she drove by.

She had scarcely turned the corner when her phone sounded with a familiar *ding*. He wanted to thank her for the evening and to let him know the next time she wanted to have drinks. Cassandra enabled the talking feature on her messages and relayed she would be available in two weeks. She also petitioned that maybe next time neither one of them had to drive anywhere after drinking. Brandon agreed to take her suggestions into consideration.

Less than two weeks later, she found herself at Brandon's favorite bar. Only minutes from her house, it boasted the opportunity for Cassandra to enact her *no drinking and driving* plan. Or at the very least, *only drive a little bit after drinking* plan. He met her outside on the patio, grinning and sporting his classic un-tucked flannel look. Conversation was light and easy. He talked, she laughed. She talked, he laughed. She wondered if life could really be that simple.

It was the final moments of the game and Brandon stood to get a better view. He sauntered up to the screen, arms crossed, prepping to raise them in victory if the right team scored the final basket. While Brandon sauntered, Cassandra caught someone else sauntering up out of the corner of her eye. "Hi, I'm Jeff. How are *you* doing today?" he asked as he offered her his hand. Jeff was older than her and perhaps a regular at the bar. Cassandra took his hand and stated she was doing well. He followed her eyes back to Brandon inquiring, "Is that your husband?"

Cassandra lowered her eyes. "No, he's...my friend."

"Oh, I see," he contended. He turned his body towards the patio door before concluding, "You know, I'm just going to go inside. Lovely to have met you Cassandra." Even through his barroom haze Jeff could see she only had eyes for Brandon.

Unaware of any actions outside the final two minutes, Brandon returned to the table where she sat. "Want to come to the tailor with me?" She nodded. Anything if it meant spending time with him.

They arrived at the parking lot at the same time, and Brandon followed her in, opening the door from behind. Chivalrous gestures were her weakness, and everything about him oozed masculinity. She mustered a coy smile as she thanked him for his thoughtful act. She caught a glimpse of his expression in the door, as she watched his smile stretch the entire length.

Cassandra busied herself with Hawaiian shirt patterns and khaki pants as Brandon located a tailor to help him with his uniform. She wandered over to the dress shirts and ties, wondering if she would ever find herself at a men's formal store under her own accord. They seemed to only exist for special occasions, and she had already cashed in on more occasions than most. With any luck maybe her next husband would be her last one, and she would come here to commemorate the occasion.

Her thoughts were interrupted as Brandon walked out of the dressing room. His pants sat loose and hung down over his feet. She smiled sweetly. There was something intimately familiar about being in such a formal setting with him. He seemed pleased to have her there as well as he flashed his signature smile over his shoulder. She hoped the next time she found herself in a place like this, it would be with someone like him.

Brandon tolerated the pulling and tugging long enough for the tailor to take the final measurements. Even routine errands were more fun with him. He held the door open for her as they walked out. "What do you want to do now?" Cassandra asked.

"I need to call my sister. It's almost nine o'clock over there." Cassandra wasn't ready for the evening to end. She still had two and a half hours of babysitting left.

She continued to work through her plan, both mentally and out loud and knew a farewell was inevitable. Sensing her hesitation or perhaps seeing no end in sight to her present conversation, Brandon leaned against the frame of her truck. “Here, why don’t we put the tailgate down?” Cassandra hopped up next to him, glad he had granted her a temporary extension.

For the next two hours, Brandon listened as she talked out her life’s ambitions, her failures and shortcomings, and where she saw her life ending up. She had goals and ambitions, but couldn’t seem to bridge the gap from her present reality. He listened with a tender sincerity as she voiced her discouragement, and squared his shoulders to offer her reassurance at just the right time. He leaned in as she spoke, satisfying her need to be heard. It made even the most discouraging outlook bearable.

Cassandra exhaled the last of her hopeless perspective, “So, what about you Brandon? Where do you see yourself ending up?” He would own a motorcycle, pack his belongings and never look back. He had a list of inventions he wanted to pursue. He would work for himself and lead a simple life. His plans didn’t mention anyone to share it with, and Cassandra wondered if he had made it that far in the planning process or if there was any room still left to apply.

***

The last five weeks had been painful, but at least at the mobilization site she could still call and text him. His final send off happened over drill weekend, and didn’t really didn’t afford Cassandra the same opportunities. It was like he had left all over again and everything seemed so permanent. She was having a hard time adjusting to her Brandon-less reality this time around. Cassandra wasn't a fan of reality television, especially this show.

With Brandon inaccessible for the next 9 months, Cassandra had to find something to pass the time. She started writing again. She threw her energy into boxing. Races were making a comeback. There were personal goals she was trying to attain, yet they were all were things that didn't involve Brandon. She wondered if there was anything she could do to bring him into her everyday life.

A journal, a daily devotional, candy and letters were all suitable items for his first care package. If she sent it now, it would be waiting for him by the time he arrived in Qatar. Cassandra knew what it was like to be deployed, and knew letters and packages were appreciated. She also knew to keep it light. Good news and milestones were always a hit. She wanted him to know he was missed, but not come on too strong. She would be the kind of friend he needed her to be.

She didn't expect to hear from him very often, or even at all. Things got busy, she understood. He wasn't that great at communicating back home, how could she really expect him to be different on deployment? She knew she would just need to find solace in her reaching out to him without expectations. Maybe a schedule would help keep her on track. She could send him a package once a month and could fill in the gaps with weekly email updates. Cassandra's phone dinged, reminding her she wouldn't see his name across her screen for quite some time.

Cassandra added *care packages* to her monthly list of things to accomplish. She even included other items she thought he might enjoy. Maybe she would theme each package for added creativity. She clapped her hands like a giddy school girl; it would be like they were working together again, except he just wouldn't be there.

Care packages were one thing, everyday life was another. Everyday life was the piece she was still trying to figure out. It was great to have goals, and for Cassandra, it was a must. Yet she found goals did very little for her day to day routine. Goals didn't give her any more time in the day to do laundry, nor did they give her any more patience with the kids. Goals didn't make her co-parenting relationship with David any better; she would need something entirely different for that and wondered why God hadn't yet let her in on that secret.

She went to church. She prayed. She talked to God. She admitted she couldn't get through the day to day grind without His help. She trusted Him…with most things. Cassandra admitted relationships were still a protected commodity, particularly her romantic ones. They were a sensitive subject. She needed to handle that herself, and would hand them over once everything else was in order, eventually. She spent so many years with the wrong people, and the one person she could see herself with was now deployed. Maybe God had gotten her order mixed up with someone else.

She found herself in church that Sunday, wondering what she needed to do to get herself back in His good graces. Maybe He hadn't heard her prayers and she needed to speak louder. Maybe He was mad and wasn't talking to her. Maybe He was too busy slapping His hand on His forehead lamenting the stupid things she had done. Whatever it was, Cassandra was convinced she had to do something differently.

The *How to Handle Uncertainty* series was of particular interest to her. How *did* you handle uncertainty, she pondered? She took out her sermon outline and a pen. She could use all of the help she could get.

The message started with the usual *give your problems to God* sort of feel, before advising folks to *prepare for God's blessings*. An *all things are possible* mantra rounded out the discussion. Cassandra watched as the pastor took out a bib and tied it around his neck. He pulled out an oversized spoon and fork from a nearby table and looked expectantly at the crowd. Cassandra waited for the punchline. "You prayed for food, now get ready. It's time to eat!"

Cassandra stared in disbelief. *Get ready. It's time to eat*. She wondered how long she had been sitting at the table of life without any utensils. She looked around as people began to make their way to the stage, laying 3 X 5" cards down as acts of surrender. Cassandra looked at her own card. She was ready to leave this one behind, and made her way to the front as she burst into tears. It had been a long road, one she didn't wish to travel down any longer.

Cassandra sobbed in the arms of the lead pastor as he prayed that even David wasn't irredeemable. God could help him too. He prayed over the relationship and prayed over Cassandra as she felt a warm sensation course through her body. Then all at once she felt her anxiety and pent up fear drain from her head down to the soles of her feet. She felt hollow, as if she had been gutted and all of the icky parts removed. Cassandra sobbed all the way back to her seat and through the length of the service. She sobbed all of the way to the bathroom and through the final song as she went to pick up the children.

So much of her had been filled with anxiety, self-doubt and other people's problems. It weighed heavily on Cassandra's heart and had sucked her soul dry. She didn't know what it was like to live in the present. So much of her life was consumed in the past. Now there was room inside for other things, like her relationships, her hopes and dreams, her kids. Her kids were the ones Cassandra thought had suffered the most.

She watched in quiet admiration as Hunter and Heather dashed across the lobby for donuts. Cassandra was fooling herself thinking her energy alone had been responsible for their enthusiasm, or even capable of taking it away. Children were the closest thing to divine intervention she had experienced in her life. Maybe God *had* given her someone to love her. Maybe He loved her so much He gave her *two* of them. Maybe God's love was right in front of her the whole time and she never even knew it, and maybe Brandon wasn't the only one who needed to learn its lesson.

***

Working full time, raising tiny humans and attempting to be civil to David was all very exhausting. It was David's "week" to have the kids and Cassandra needed to recharge. Cassandra's "week" would begin the stroke after daycare on Friday and last through the following weekend. It was ten days for her, four days for him. All weekends for her and only week days for him. It was practically the same, at least from David's perspective. He didn't understand why she was so tired all of the time.

Thursday would be her lucky day. For some, luck fell into their lap with little effort. For Cassandra, it had to be planned two weeks ahead of time to ensure all of her bases were covered. There was the meal. She would need child care coverage. First time guests received a tour of a clean home. She needed to give herself enough time to mentally prepare for guests over the age of four. It was all very important, and time was running out. She would pop the question after their Monday morning meeting. With any luck, the evening would stretch into the night, and give Cassandra a chance to try out her home away from home theory.

Cassandra was on track for Thursday when Tuesday threw her a curveball. He didn't like going out during the week. The weekend would be more conducive to his schedule. The weekends meant children. She had chosen a week day on purpose and she wanted it to be just the two of them. The only saving grace was that Heather would be asleep and

Hunter could help with the food. Cassandra sighed and threw the pork roast in the freezer.

For every act she completed, four little hands undid them with twice the speed. As expected, Heather went to sleep and Hunter helped prepare the meal. He helped chop the salad, roll the biscuits and prepare the main crock pot dish. Whoever said *many hands makes light work*, didn't have toddlers running around their home. Little hands wanted to help. Little hands also wanted to throw toys all over the clean floor. "Noooo, please!" Cassandra pleaded. "I just want him to see the house clean *once*!" Cassandra sprang from the floor to the oven, as she pulled the biscuits out with ten minutes to spare. She used the final few minutes to compose herself before her guest arrived.

Cassandra alerted the media that her friend would be coming and would be driving a white truck. Hunter pressed his face to the glass to get a better look. It was two o'clock and Brandon hadn't arrived yet. He must be running late. She would give him a few more minutes before she asked him where he was. A familiar *ding* echoed down the hall. She scanned his message as she picked up the phone. *I went to meet my buddy and I'm running a little late. I will be there closer to three.* Cassandra's jaw tightened. She was his friend too. Didn't *her* time count for anything? Her face began to redden. Maybe it was a good thing he was running late, she needed time to cool off.

She grabbed a book from Hunter's collection. She didn't know that *I Love You Forever* could be given an angry rendition. Even still, Hunter crawled on her lap for story time. Cassandra was both annoyed and touched that he saw her as a place of refuge. The story did nothing to fuel her rage so she picked up *Lilo and Stitch*. Stitch's destructive personality would surely deliver. She was distracted from her anger just long enough to be sucked back in as Hunter peered out the window. "Where's you friend? He not coming?" Cassandra's heart rate began to rise as she checked her watch. It was three-thirty. She knew where she stood on his priority list. The only thing that would be more irritating would be if he were dead, Cassandra thought. In that moment she cared more about the food going to waste than his non-existence. But just to make sure, she sent him a text. ETA was still fifteen minutes out. Now she had permission to continue her homicidal storyline.

Hunter jumped up as a white truck pulled in front of their house. "He's here!" he yelled as he ran to the door. He was an hour and forty-five minutes late. If Heather wasn't up by now, Cassandra was sure she would be soon, and she wouldn't get any time alone with him. The biscuits were probably cold. He was probably worn out from his trip and likely had little left to give her. This was supposed to be her day to rejuvenate. Instead, she spent it policing up clothes and toys from the floor and cooking a dinner people didn't care enough about to show up on time for. She wished he had just stayed home.

Cassandra settled back into her book and didn't bother to get up. She would make him wait like he made her wait. The front door opened and she heard Hunter issue a greeting. She rolled her eyes. Now she was obligated to talk to him.

She would offer a pouty greeting. The silent treatment was always a crowd favorite. Brandon found his way to the kitchen, undoubtedly looking for Cassandra, but she wasn't sure she was ready to talk to him. She entered the room to find him staring out the sliding door into the backyard. He looked defeated, and Cassandra fought to hold on to her anger as she made her way towards him. She tightened her fists and clenched her jaw, he needed to know how she felt. She peered into his eyes as she approached, but was sure he already knew. She unclenched her hand and offered a stiff, "You made it."

Brandon shook his head in disbelief. It had been quite the day. Cassandra's gaze softened and she wrapped her arms around him. Maybe he just needed a hug. He turned his body to the side and began to pull away in discomfort. Beginning of the day hugs weren't really in his script. Hugs weren't written in until the farewell scene. Perhaps realizing that maybe he really did need that hug, Brandon relaxed his body and sighed deeply into her embrace. Cassandra could feel the relief wash over him. "I'm sorry," he breathed into her hair. Cassandra's heart softened. It seemed both of them needed that hug.

"Lunch is ready," she offered. "Are you hungry?"

He followed her to the kitchen, leaning over her shoulder as she offered her culinary tour. "Is there anything I can help with?" he asked expectantly.

Cassandra handed him a cutting board and knife. "Cut the roast for me, please?" The pork roast slid off the fork before he could even rescue it from the simmering crockpot.

Brandon breathed in her culinary creation. "It smells good," he exhaled as he panned the room.

"Where do you usually sit?" Cassandra gestured to the sturdy oak table behind them. Bar stools at the kitchen counter were also an option. He placed the plates on the counter and pulled her barstool next to him. She smiled. It was almost like a date.

Two tiny eyes peered at her over the barstool. That was Hunter's favorite spot. She pulled up a chair from the table behind them and patted the seat on the other side of her as Hunter excitedly climbed aboard. As Cassandra darted around for drink orders, extra napkins and unique toddler flavor requests, she began to feel the stress that parenting and entertaining promised. Hunter was only half of the equation. She hadn't heard from Heather for hours. Maybe she should go check on her. She rushed to the edge of the counter as she caught Brandon's eye. Maybe Heather could wait just a few more minutes.

Despite tiny interested onlookers, Cassandra and Brandon managed to talk about life. They talked about life before and after deployment, life goals and ambitions and recent life realizations. As she at last sat down to eat, Brandon helped clear the dishes away and rinse them in the sink. She watched in amazement as he lifted up her and her son's plate to clean under them with a sponge. It was his turn to wait on her. She smiled. He was worth the wait.

Cassandra turned to look at the clock. She couldn't believe Heather was still asleep. Her fears of not being able to have an adult conversation were suddenly replaced with fears of little people not being able to sleep through the night. "I should go wake her up," Cassandra contended. "Not sure what your plans are the rest of the day…but I was wondering if you'd like to go the park with us. It's right down the street."

His signature smile tugged at the edges of his mouth as he replied, "Sure."

Cassandra pulled the wagon behind her as she walked next to him. By his side was one of her favorite places, and his manliness made it all the more enjoyable. It wasn't long before they arrived at the park and the children scattered across the playground. Hunter headed towards the basketball hoop, with Brandon on his heels. Cassandra chased Heather up one tractor slide and down the other. She glanced towards the basketball courts just as Brandon picked up Hunter for a basket. She watched as smiles erupted on both of their faces and they exchanged a high five. The last of Cassandra's lunchtime disappointment vanished. He was playing with her son and she never asked him to. As Brandon made his way over, Cassandra's reverence spilled over into a hug.

True to his aversion to middle of the day affection, Brandon stepped to the side and passed it off as a one armed embrace. His arm hung loosely around her shoulder as he turned his attention towards Hunter. Cassandra blushed. Perhaps she had been a little over zealous. She wondered if she still had time to pass it off as playful. As she pulled away, she felt Brandon's arm tighten around her shoulder. Not sure if she had imagined it or if it was an invitation to continue, she slipped her arm around his waist. His heartbeat quickened in her ear, and she felt his breath graze her cheek. It was definitely an invitation and her body melted into his. As Hunter zigzagged excitedly from one hiding place to another, contentment stretched across her face. What she wouldn't give to have this be her life.

They walked side by side to a nearby bridge as Cassandra anticipated her next Brandon Fletcher moment. Wondering how she might arrange such a thing, she turned excitedly to the kids and asked, "Want to throw some sticks and rocks in the water?" Cheers erupted from the wagon as they threw open the door and ran underneath the trees. They followed as the children desperately searched for something to throw into the water. Their excavation was noticed by a man taking his dog for a walk. He was the second person to assume Brandon and Cassandra were together, and that it was family day at the park. Neither of them corrected him, and followed Hunter and Heather to their preferred launching spot.

Brandon leaned on the crossbeams of the bridge while the kids added to their collection. Sensing another invitation, Cassandra leaned on her elbows next to him. Her inner school girl playfully nudged his arm. He grinned in her direction and offered a new conversation. Even in the middle of sticks and rocks being hurled overhead, the conversation took on a very *life plans* sort of direction. Those were Cassandra's favorite topics. Brandon brought them up often, especially since news of the deployment. Often he was curious about her plans in his absence and when he returned. He never said so directly, but Cassandra felt like he was sizing her up. Maybe that was his way of seeing if they would be compatible when he got back. She often wondered if he saw her in his plans.

The walk home yielded a detour and more of the same introspective speech. He didn't offer advice on life very often but when he did, Cassandra made it a point to follow it to a tee. He suggested she watch *Good Luck Chuck*. It was entertaining, and she might be able to relate. It didn't sound like her kind of movie, but Brandon would never lead her astray. She added it to her list of must dos.

They were rounding the corner to her house when the wagon hit a bump in the sidewalk. Cassandra pulled and tugged. She tried again as the stiff suspension threatened to tip it. She looked expectantly at Brandon. "Can you help me?" In a single thrust, he dislodged the wagon and they continued on their way. Cassandra would be lying if she said she didn't notice the view from behind as he pulled the wagon. Although it was with its own advantages, she much more preferred his face. The day had been amazing, she hoped he knew that.

Home meant ice cream and a movie for little people. For Cassandra, it meant that the day was winding down and Brandon would soon be on his way. She needed to squeeze the last few moments out of her afternoon. With the ice cream and movie diversion in place, Brandon settled in across from her at the high top table. Deciding he could do without theme music, he got up and Cassandra followed him back to the kitchen barstools. She had seen that look before. His shields were down, and the man sitting before her was the real Brandon Fletcher. This version of him lived in the present moment and was in touch with his feelings. And from what she could see, those feelings were largely sentimental, and clearly associated with her.

"I better get going," Brandon at last concluded. Cassandra could sense his hesitation. Her house had felt like a home with him in it. He moved around with a familiarity and sense of comfort that seemed characteristic of their whole relationship. He definitely knew her better than anyone else, and she was acquainted with him more than most. Even though he didn't say it, she knew few people were permitted that level of entry into his life. His whole life he had built a wall around his heart. He now helped Cassandra tear down a corner before putting it back up. She watched the view from inside the walls now. He was the love of her life. She wondered if he could ever accept that. Brandon searched her eyes as she contemplated his heart. He followed her into the kitchen as she surveyed the remains of the afternoon.

"Do you want any of this to take home with you?" Cassandra asked. Pork was his favorite. She could see his hesitation.

He paused a moment longer before replying, "No thanks." He leaned up against the kitchen counter. "Thank you for lunch." Cassandra leaned into him and felt the familiar weight of his head resting on hers. Brandon pulled back and found her eyes. He squeezed her shoulders and ran his hands up and down her arms. Cassandra thought she was done with the embrace until he touched her arms. Unable to control herself, she launched back in. If she was a cat she would have purred. His arms were definitely her happy place.

They separated just long enough to walk back into the other room. But like tiny magnets pulling them together, they soon found themselves back in each other's arms. Brandon peered over her shoulder to find a pair of scrunched up eyes staring at him. "Don't take it personally. It's all men," Cassandra contended. "The only ones she doesn't mind are the ones she's related to." Still in her embrace, Brandon turned them both to get a clearer picture of Heather before countering, "Well you're going to have a hard time getting married then!"

"Don't tell her that!" Cassandra teased.

"Well it's true!" he mused.

With a final goodbye to Hunter, Brandon slipped out of her arms and once again thanked her for the day. His eyes threatened to pull her back in, but Cassandra resisted. Five hugs were probably enough. She couldn't believe he had let her hug him so many times. I *must be wearing him down*, she thought. He was so amazing. He fit into their lives seamlessly and Cassandra seriously considered extending him a permanent invitation. He had already been asked twice, perhaps the third time would be the charm for both of them.

***

A 50,000 word challenge. Cassandra stared down the corridor of doubt, unsure if her talent would be enough to pull her through. She found herself in the first week of National Novel Writing Month and she was already behind. November drill threw her into the red with OPORD hangover. Now she desperately tried to make up for the deficit she had incurred. Why did she even want to do it, she wondered? Bragging rights? To say that she did it? To force some discipline into her unstructured life? And what if she didn't finish?

50,000 words in 30 days. That amounted to roughly 12,500 words a week. 1,667 words a day. Did titles or chapter names count? The experts advised to just write without regard to content. Silencing the inner critic would be the key. If her inner critic had some good ideas, waiting until the end to release them may hamper her efforts. Where would she even start? She missed Brandon. Maybe she would start there.

Writing about Brandon had to be perfect. If not perfect, just palatable to the human eye. Cassandra thought long and hard. How could she even begin to describe her relationship with him? It was complex and dynamic, not to mention confusing and hard to explain. She paused. Was she writing for herself or because someone had suggested she give it a try? She always enjoyed writing, maybe she could learn to enjoy structured discipline too. She would start with the final goodbye, and work her way back from there.

Brandon was her favorite topic so Cassandra naturally assumed writing about him would be effortless. If effortless meant stifled and superficial, she was right on track. She was practically born with a pen in right hand and journal in her left, yet years had passed since she wrote with any great frequency. Motherhood seemed to have stamped out the last of her creativity. Sure, there were letters, emails and the occasional riveting operations order, but those were merely snapshots in Cassandra's life. Journaling had provided her an opportunity to play investigator, reporting from the front lines of hurt, doubt or anxiety, with the occasional good news story. The rusty wheels of creativity slowly started to turn and Cassandra soon had four hundred words pen to paper, rather computer to paper. Only forty-nine and a half thousand to go, she thought.

And that was another thing too; the word count. How often was she supposed to check? Every few sentences? Every paragraph? Maybe it was like the treadmill; where you only looked when you needed encouragement to keep going. This was harder than Cassandra thought. Maybe she wasn't up for the challenge, or maybe she just needed a little encouragement from her inner critic.

How much time would she need to set aside every day to accomplish this goal? Between work and the kids, how would she manage yet another commitment? Would she be a failure if she didn't finish? Would she have enough ideas to sustain a 50,000 word beast or would she run out half way through? What if she didn't have enough life experiences to effectively draft a best seller? Inner critic never failed to deliver, but at least now she would have plenty to get started.

She wanted to paint a loving picture of Brandon and couldn't talk about the bad stuff; like his anger, or his incessant complaining or even his inability to believe in love. Divorce hadn't exactly been easy either, but she couldn't let people know just how much she cared about Brandon because she didn't want their friendship tarnished with accusations. She would leave all editing until the end, yet every typo and misused word jumped out on the page like eyesores. She couldn't ask readers to believe a story she wasn't fully invested in herself. Cassandra ran her cursor back over the glaring errors and smoothed out the rough edges. She cocked her head to the side and read it again. She had to do Brandon's story justice, after all, it was her story too.

It was her story of heartache and disappointment. Of doubt and anxiety. Of love and longing. Cassandra hadn't been allowed to feel love or anything else for the past few years. Her feelings were always wrong and came after David's. She certainly wasn't allowed to feel affection for Brandon. That much she did know. Except that she did feel it, and she had felt it for a long time. Cassandra wondered if that made her a bad person. David thought so. Every time she thought about Brandon a pang of guilt pulled at her heartstrings. Maybe she really was an adulteress. Maybe her readers needed to decide for themselves.

The first few days of the novel writing challenge were as its title suggested; challenging. Finding the time to write was the biggest challenge. Cassandra was relegated to borrowing against the workday just to make literary ends meet. Then there was the matter of still being behind from those first few days. Cassandra's brain was overwhelmed at the thought of producing twice the volume of words per day just to stay on track. Her writing was reduced to a painful type, check, type, check battle rhythm. She let the number of words drive her mood and her achievements. The scrolling word count at the bottom of the page was like her guilty addiction. She couldn't help staring at it, hoping that each increase would bring greater satisfaction and euphoria than the last as she skyrocketed to her goal.

Cassandra's writing was largely devoid of feeling, except the parts containing accounts of Brandon. Her readers definitely picked up on her affections for him, David not so much. The "in-between" moments as Cassandra called them were just something to fill the time until the next Brandon encounter. Passive voice abounded, and Cassandra's connection to her feelings was like a short circuited electrical current. Sometimes the reader got her inner thoughts and turmoil, and sometimes they didn't. She had to pace herself.

Every time she wrote at work she felt a sense of anxiety rising, like she was doing something she knew she shouldn't be doing. She was mismanaging government resources. Yet, it wasn't like Cassandra's work center was overflowing. After the brigade level exercise last year and the push to get folks out the door for the mobilization, her own battle rhythm slowed down exponentially. October and November drill caused it to spike, but steady state operations were in effect and clear waters were evident. Cassandra's work life balance had been skewed for an extended amount of time, maybe it was just trying to find that balance that peaked her insecurities. Cassandra only wrote in her free time. Once drill concluded, she just happened to have a lot more of it than she realized.

Cassandra did everything she could to stimulate mental production. She wrote from her kitchen table. She wrote from her desk. She would stand. She would sit. She would crack open a cider. Anything to activate the sensors in her brain to think in a different way. She would take days off of work and binge on boxing and writing. She would write at work. She would write at home after the kids went to bed. She wrote an outline of high points she wanted to visit. At one point she finally stopped looking at her word count and stopped trying to make the challenge.

30 days wasn't the challenge, she concluded, it was finishing. Her story would be told, it just might take closer to 45 or 60 days to finish relating. Cassandra set her own word count and realistic time frame for completion. She was going to do it. She would write every day. As Cassandra reread her work, there were definite flavors that existed throughout the manuscript. She could almost tell what kind of mood she was in when she wrote it. She wondered if her readers would be able to piece it together.

Cassandra was coming into her own as a writer, or maybe she had always been there and just needed a little reminder. She was pleased with her work and what she was able to piece together. Writing gave her a chance to explore her feelings, and if Cassandra was being honest with herself, she struggled to recall a time where she felt truly loved. People had certainly loved her, but seemed to have always come with a price. Her parents. Her co-workers. Her significant other. The only people she felt came close to displaying any type of unconditional affections were her friends. Cassandra thought back through the years. Her own family had often made her feel judged.

It was never malicious or even intentional, yet familial judgment had taken on many subtle forms throughout the years. A look, a sarcastic comment, a well-placed jab when she was already feeling low. Downplaying her abilities or judging her emotions. Over a lifetime it added up. When the criticism wasn't replaced with something more encouraging, it became her only identity. Cassandra often over compensated by throwing herself into work and accomplishing goals for the organization. The Army was great for her personality; it gave her purpose and direction. Yet the mission was done. The war was over. Cassandra had no purpose or direction. She wondered if that was the real cause of her unhappiness.

She was waiting for the team to stabilize at work so she could get new marching orders. She was waiting for Brandon to get back so she could have more direction in her life. She was waiting for her ex-husband to stop being a jerk so they could co-parent. She was waiting for the kids to grow out of their temperamental stage so she would stop feeling so taxed. She was waiting for God to snap out of it and throw her a bone. The only person Cassandra hadn't waited on was herself. She pushed herself away from the keyboard. Maybe the problem wasn't everyone else. Maybe it was her.

Her head began to reel. Had she really been the cause of her own problems? God had been silent through her divorce and threw her some occasional scraps to keep the plot going, but what if the plot line was of her own doing? Cassandra was waiting for God to snap out of it, maybe He was waiting on the same from her. She wondered if He really *did* have blessings He wanted to throw her way and she was too busy looking down to notice?

Cassandra studied the rolodex of her mind and searched the last few years. She had never had much luck attracting a suitable partner. Of the ones she did attract and wound up marrying, they never quite hit the mark. Neither one was her type. Cassandra had always blamed the worldwide shortage and had blamed God for not wanting her to be happy. She later determined it was up to her to be happy, and she would simply try to make the most out of her unequally yoked decisions. No one had forced her to marry David or Dewayne. They were decisions of her own free will; decisions largely influenced by her lack of significant relationships and her desire to have children. Each seemed like the best option in their respective eras, but neither one was complete within themselves. Each seemed to offer Cassandra a piece of what she was missing. Neither one fit her definition of a life partner, but she was pressed for time. She needed to be happy with what was available to her. True love was for more deserving people.

Up until this point, Cassandra had wavered on her decision to date. Her biggest objection had been not wanting to betray Brandon, but it wasn't like men were exactly lined up around the block to meet her either. She quickly dismissed this option. Obstacle number two was David. How could she find love in a relationship when David was lurking around every corner wanting to steal her joy like some troll under a bridge? Her co-parenting model was already precariously balanced, adding anyone else might cause her to lose what little traction she had obtained.

Her only task for the last nine months was repeatedly putting the same puzzle pieces together over and over again. She didn't have the energy to rebuild anything else. *She didn't have the energy. Obstacle number three.* She was exhausted. What did she hope to provide a new partner?

Thinking about Brandon had become more exciting than her day to day life. She could look back and relive the moments over and over again as he offered her a glimpse into his world. His text messages were her favorite bedtime story. When she wasn't busy thinking about all of the amazing memories they shared, she could fast forward and busy herself with all of the events that were yet to come. This took up most of her available energy pool. What energy she did have left Cassandra divided between her kids and her normal household and vocational duties. Her kids often ended up at the shallow end of her available pool. Brandon had gotten her through her divorce, and up until this point, Cassandra thought that he needed to be the one to get her through the deployment too. He was the focus, and everything and *everyone* else had been distractions.

Cassandra closed the laptop and walked to the other room. Had her life really been a lie post-divorce? Maybe not so much a lie as it had happened without her participation. She could definitely see the places where she had firmly dug her heels in. Life had definitely happened. The kids definitely existed. Work definitely continued. Maybe Cassandra had just been too bogged down with life to notice the series of opportunities along the way. Novel Writing Month had been one of them. Kickboxing classes was another. Races were sprinkled in for an added morale boost. Even her children revealed moments of joy. She didn't have to wait for Brandon to get back to start life, it could start right now, even in his absence. But how would she get there?

Cassandra thought back to her experiences after Brandon left. The kickboxing, the writing and the races had all brought her joy and allowed her to burn off some steam. She hadn't engaged in any of those activities *until* Brandon left. Maybe his leaving was the catalyst for her to learn to be okay on her own. Maybe it *was* okay to have fun without him. Maybe that was okay too. Maybe everything *was* okay, and it was Cassandra that was out of balance.

***

Time was running out this side of deployment, and Brandon's next milestone would be his pre-deployment site visit, just one month away from mobilization. His schedule would undoubtedly be filling up soon, and Cassandra would need to book availability now. She was trying not to be desperate, but couldn't help feeling that time was slipping away from her. Fundamentally, she knew he was leaving. Even still, she found herself grabbing onto every available moment. He would be leaving soon, and she didn't know if he was even coming back.

A deployment to Qatar was relatively safe as deployments go, it wasn't even considered a combat zone. What was unclear was Brandon's plans post-deployment. He had sold his home. He wanted to quit the military. He wanted to move back to the Midwest.

He wanted to fall off the grid and live out his days gold panning in seclusion. He wanted to do away with his cell phone so no one could contact him. Yet he had also applied for a contracting job in Salem with the Army Corp of Engineers. He subleased his apartment so he would have somewhere to stay when he got back. He had a friend hold onto his truck. He wanted to leave the unit for a lower stress military occupation. Brandon' life plan was anything but constant.

Cassandra knew she couldn't stop the mobilization, nor did she want to. He needed this. Maybe if she held on a little longer he might reveal his future plans to her. If she played her cards right, maybe he would even let her be a part of them. Even if she couldn't physically be with Brandon for the deployment, just knowing that he was there and would be coming back to her would be enough. She couldn't think about that now, deployment was still a month away.

Despite his in-demand status, Cassandra's secretary managed to book Brandon for drinks the following Thursday. She knew his time was precious. He *was* a company commander after all. He was also her friend, one of her closest. She knew he would make time for her. Time was precious to him, and maybe she was too.

Cassandra was a little late leaving the office as she made her way across the downtown traffic. She entered the pub to find Brandon sitting at a high top table for two. A signature smile erupted on his face as she sat down. "I'm glad you're here," he offered. "Now we can finally order." Cassandra playfully rolled her eyes. He always knew what to say to touch her heart.

First came appetizers and drinks. Next came stories and banter. There were of course the normal *works sucks, I can't believe how this is going* tales of bravery and perseverance, later evolving into the *what are your goals this next year?* sort of conversation that had been staples since the deployment had become a thing. His tone seemed lighter than usual, and for once disgust and disappointment were not key ingredients to the interchange. Brandon seemed focused on the experience itself rather than promoting his personal beliefs on life. It was different than what Cassandra was used to. She wanted to take this version of Brandon on a test drive.

He had something he wanted to show her, and Cassandra leaned over in anxious anticipation. It was a video on millennials. Brandon could barely steady himself long enough to hold the phone for Cassandra before he burst out laughing. Next were snippets from bogus talk shows and stand-up routines. Brandon's eyes beamed across the table. Humor was a good look for him. She wondered if this is what he would be like on a date.

The idea of Brandon on a date was intriguing to Cassandra. If Brandon was an action figure, she wondered what would be his signature move. Would it be uttering witty one-liners during inappropriate parts of the conversations? Maybe there be a button you could push that would allow his hand to come up and deflect certain parts of the conversation. Maybe his action figure would come equipped with delayed kissing action. Would it come standard with joke making ability, or would it need to be purchased separately? Cassandra smirked. She would definitely buy one.

Brandon raised his hand and hailed, "Check please. *One* check, please." Cassandra wasn't used to having people pay for things. Her father had taught her the importance of pulling your own weight, and tensed as the check passed in front of her. Her father had also taught her the importance of chivalry and accepting other's generosity. Cassandra pulled back. Brandon placed a sequence of bills on top before nodding in her direction, "Now let's get out of here."

Buying her drinks was one of those things he did that made her feel unmistakably feminine. Opening doors was another. Letting her walk in front of him was almost too much for her. Maybe it was just him. Maybe he was such a man that everything he did exerted masculine energy. It had been so long since she had felt feminine. He was beautiful. He made her feel beautiful. She wondered if he knew just how much he meant to her.

Brandon paused mid-stride to show her another talk show video. He leaned in close to give her a good view of the screen. The content of the video was irrelevant. It could have been about a space alien abduction for all Cassandra was concerned. The only thing she was paying attention to was him and how close he was to her. She could hear him breathing as she watched his chest rise and fall. She desperately wanted to put her arm around him and was sure he wouldn't mind. Yet she resisted her pheromone induced urges and left her arm planted by her side. She would keep her hands to herself tonight.

A few moments later, Brandon paused again for a mock counseling session. What Cassandra wouldn't give to throw him on the sidewalk and make love to him. She was sure the local authorities would object, and probably the small children playing baseball across the way. Their parents probably would too. A group of people would start forming on the street and impede traffic. Disgruntled motorists would leave tire marks in the grass trying to go around. People would be angry and stage a protest. It was probably best if she just kept her hands to herself, but it was Brandon though, it was a pretty tall order.

The night was winding down, and Brandon stopped to offer his closing comments on the evening. One hug never seemed like enough. After the fourth one he started to get a little antsy. "Good lord woman!" he exclaimed. "I *will* see you tomorrow." Cassandra paused in slight embarrassment. No he wouldn't. She was out of the office. The next time he would see her would be in two weeks, after his pre deployment site visit. She was simply resolving a supply and demand issue.

"Be safe. See you when you get back," Cassandra uttered as Brandon slowly began to back away.

"Yes you will," Brandon replied as he met her eyes. He took a few more steps back before he turned around. Cassandra watched as he snuck a peek over his shoulder in her direction. She would never get used to him leaving, no matter how much she enjoyed the view.

***

"Mommy, why you no like Daddy anymore?"

Cassandra cast a gentle glance in the direction of her son. It seemed like a pretty heavy order for bedtime. She found herself completely unprepared to answer the question so she repeated it. "Why don't I like Daddy anymore?" Hunter's face nodded in the glow of the night light.

The parenting class seemed like a lifetime ago. What could she possibly tell a four year old about divorce in a way that he would understand? Cassandra began, "Mommy likes Daddy. Sometimes people just…they just don't get along and have to do things by themselves."

"What mean Mommy?"

Cassandra continued. "You know how you and Heather don't always get along? Like sometimes she wants to do one thing and you want to do something else?" She paused as he nodded. "Sometimes grown-ups need to have their own space so they can do the things they want to do. Does that make sense? Do you understand sweetheart?"

"I understand."

"Even though Mommy and Daddy live in different houses, they still love you and Heather, and want to do everything to take care of you." That much Cassandra *had* remembered from the parenting class.

"Mommy, why 'Chell no like Daddy anymore? Why no one come to visit Daddy's house anymore?"

Cassandra was unprepared for quiz time. She sighed. "Chell likes Daddy, she just doesn't see him very much."

"Why?"

"Because Daddy needs a special key to get into his apartment, and only Daddy has the key to it." A secured building was a definite obstacle to entertaining, but Cassandra knew it was only half of the equation. With his half explanation, Hunter happily shoved his dinosaur book into Cassandra's face. They had left off on gigantic dinosaurs. She had skirted further conversation tonight, but something told her she wouldn't always be so lucky. She was just glad Heather didn't understand cause and effect yet.

Bedtime snores echoed from the pillow next to her as she placed the *Little Book of Giant Dinosaurs* on Hunter's headrest. It was time for her to go to sleep too, and tonight she could use it. She slipped into her pajama pants and removed her flannel to reveal her *Miller-Fletcher Center for Logistical Excellence* t-shirt. She practically lived in it. It was her favorite. What started out as a juvenile taunt from her supervisor soon became a trademark and a symbol of their partnership, both in and out of the logistical arena. It became a source of comfort for Cassandra, especially not knowing Brandon's fate post-deployment.

More than just a t-shirt, it was the idea that something bonded them together. No matter what his fate, it was like a little piece of him would always be with her. They started something together, and maybe the t-shirt was Cassandra's way of believing he would come back for her. She wondered if he had taken his with him and if he thought of her when he wore it. Maybe it was locked up in the bottom of a black box on a container across the ocean. Maybe it had been hijacked by Somali pirates and her copy was the only surviving memorabilia of the logistical institute they created together. Both of their shirts sported *Founding Member* across the back like a team jersey, and their Battalion Commander had been the first to graduate from the institute. In jest, her Commander had called them a two headed monster. Cassandra would be a monster, if it meant being close to Brandon.

Cassandra sighed as her head hit the pillow. Qatar was ten hours ahead and Brandon no doubt would be up for the day and moving around. They were like two ships passing in the night. She imagined high fiving him as she came off of the night shift and he was there to relieve her. Why did deployments have to be so long? Furthermore, why did she have to fall for someone that the universe was playing keep away with? Cassandra needed to turn her brain off. It was bedtime.

She closed her eyes as her thoughts drifted to moments spent with Brandon, and those to come. She replayed the good-bye as she pictured him boarding the plane. She imagined him opening her letter and feeling like someone of significance to have received mail from such an adoring fan. She fast forwarded to the demobilization ceremony. It was an experience starkly similar to the first, except this one involved a hug with a twirl at the end, and a less than subdued Brandon gazing into her eyes gently pressing his lips to hers. He would smile his impish grin and act as though it was embarrassing and he didn't want anyone to see, yet would proudly show her off as someone of significance. He would look into her eyes and ask her what she was doing later. She would calmly reply, *that's up to you.*

The demobilization ceremony would likely be on a weekend to promote maximum attendance. That meant she would need to secure babysitting. They wouldn't be able to go back to her place because that's where her kids would likely be, unless her sister volunteered to take them back to her place so Cassandra could have some time alone with Brandon. They would engage in passionate lovemaking. He would study her eyes with every move, sighing softly as she touched his body. Cassandra wondered what type of lover he would be. He was detail oriented and meticulous. She reasoned he would be the slow and sensual type.

Cassandra's fantasy began to take a turn from PG-13 into adult content when she felt the bed move next to her. Through the darkness she saw Hunter repositioning himself on the mattress, dragging his blanket from his bed as he had been instructed to do on previous occasions. Every night he came to visit, and Cassandra anticipated his arrival with well placed pillows and extra blankets to protect against the perils of toddlerhood. She reached over and took his hand. She felt his fingers grip hers, and he soon drifted back into sleep. He had come to her for protection and safety. Everything was better with Mommy. Cassandra understood and stopped trying to fight against the invasion. She knew what it was like to seek comfort in someone else's presence. She knew entirely too well how it was to want.

She wondered what it would be like when Brandon was laying in the bed next to her for real. How would Hunter react? He would have started school by then. Would he still be coming to her bed every night? Much like *The Three Bears*, Cassandra wondered how Hunter would react to somebody *lying in my bed*! How would he react at all to any relationship Cassandra would find herself in? She often wondered if he, or anyone else for that matter, would authorize it. The conversation was getting too heavy for a Tuesday night. Cassandra vowed to pick this up on her morning commute.

It had been two months since Brandon left. If she was in a support group she would have received a coin for her efforts. Surely there was some group out there that would support her cause. Traffic definitely didn't support her cause, it didn't even need her to be present to occur. Others tried to support her cause knowing the difficulties she would face. With Brandon removed from the picture, her co-workers and acquaintances were doing their best to reach out. Perhaps Cassandra had just not been in a place to appreciate it while Brandon was here. Maybe his departure was an invitation to examine the world she had missed.

She didn't miss Brandon any less, she was just getting used to a world without his constant interaction. Calling and texting were no longer an option. She sent him letters and emails wanting him to know she was thinking about him. Cassandra knew not to expect replies right away or even at all sometimes, he was deployed and schedules weren't always consistent. She got it but still, she couldn't help but anticipate something. The smallest email reply would send her mood to record highs. Even if the theme was anger and frustration over the day's events, Cassandra took heart because he had thought to include her in his daily duties. She knew a high operational tone was not conducive to sentimental flow. She knew not to be disappointed. She knew he held her in high regard.

The holidays were approaching and Cassandra tossed around ideas on how to make them more meaningful for Brandon. While he never seemed to identify very strongly with special occasions this side of the Atlantic, there was something different about deployment. There was something about deployment that gave you permission to miss home, as well as all of the traditions that may or may not have occurred in the past. It was a time to reflect on what your life was and what you wanted it to become. It was a time to establish a new way forward. *Establishing a new way forward*, maybe that was what this deployment meant to Cassandra too.

***

Cassandra paced back and forth as she peered out the window into the crowded parking lot. 30 pieces of rolling stock were slated to go to California and all but half a dozen stared expectantly back at her. Training was scheduled to start in two days. Cassandra didn't know much about contracting, but she knew enough to not hire this vendor again. They "promised" to have all of the equipment there before training started. But then again, they had said that two days ago, and another three days before that. *Perfect*, she thought. She was the officer in charge of this mission. It hadn't even officially begun yet and already seemed to be off on the wrong foot. Cassandra felt her phone vibrate in her pocket. It was Brandon. At least there would be one thing that could go right with this day.

In the months nearing deployment, Cassandra had come to accept Brandon's departure as eminent, and as such, she began to loosen her grip on the demand to spend time with him. She knew his schedule was tight. She said her final goodbyes after drill last month, and thought that would be the last time until the mobilization ceremony that she would be able to speak her peace. The more Cassandra let go, the more Brandon seemed available to reminisce. They had clocked in quite a few work time lunches. There were the impromptu "life" speeches in each others' office. Today offered a slight variation.

"Hello?" Cassandra answered as she tried to stifle a smile.

"Hey," Brandon offered as his customary response. It felt familiar and comfortable. Cassandra loved it. "I went to your office to talk to you but I couldn't find you. Where are you?"

"I came downstairs to see Sergeant Thomas about the line haul. Apparently only like six trucks have left. It's crazy."

"I didn't want to leave before I had a chance to talk to you." *Oh?* Cassandra thought. He had her undivided attention. "I'm leaving here soon. I know you wanted to meet up, but I didn't want to leave without touching base with you."

"Are you still in your office?"

"Yes. I'm leaving in about 30 minutes."

"Okay, stand by. I'm making my way over there now." Cassandra hung up the phone and headed down the hall.

Although he had just spoken to her minutes before, Brandon greeted her with eyes wide, gasping softly as she entered the room. He had been doing that lately. Cassandra preferred to think it was because her presence made him as tingly as his made her, but she didn't want to get her hopes up. She would just contend he had eaten something unsettling for lunch and needed to take an extra breath to calm his stomach. He grinned ear to ear. Cassandra couldn't help but return the favor.

She was never quite sure how to begin conversations with him in his office and it reminded her of being in his apartment or his house. It was his space and he had invited her into it. She was keenly aware of his male persona as it seemed to fill every corner of the crowded room. She wanted to say everything yet say nothing at all. She could live off of the alluring nature of his eyes. He was so amazing. She was soaking him in; a task she wished could somehow be substituted for his impending pre-mobilization training.

Work was always a classic so they started there. As Cassandra dove into the details of her day and the race to pre-mobilization eve, she saw Brandon looking at her with that same sort of infatuated smirk she had grown accustomed to. The teenage girl in her smiled shyly and looked away. Cassandra couldn't remember what she was talking about. Her train of thought had been completely derailed when the world's hottest guy aimed his infatuation at her. This was uncharted territory and Cassandra looked down. She was still wearing her uniform as Brandon sat comfortably in jeans and a polo. She may have outranked him, but right now it was just the two of them spending one last evening together.

Perhaps sensing her distracted thoughts, Brandon chimed in, "I'll be able to stay for about an hour. Where do you want to do this thing at?"

"I put them in the fridge in the kitchen." She had been nervous about the infraction all day. Brandon followed her out and closed the door. "We're coming back here I thought. I mean, I wasn't planning on doing it in the kitchen. It's dark in there." Brandon cocked his head to the side and unlocked the door, following her down the hall to the industrial sized kitchen.

Cassandra shuffled a few bags and boxes around to reveal a gray canvas cooler. She acquired it a few months back when she signed up for her *Costco* credit card. She had only used it once before, and somehow felt it appropriate for this occasion. She glanced over her shoulder before slinging the bag. "Let's go," she said.

She felt like she was robbing a bank, or rather walking into the bank to put back the money she had taken. The 60 second walk back to his office was excruciating. She was a Major in the United States Army. Maybe they could expect this sort of thing from Privates and lower enlisted folks, but not from her. Cassandra unzipped the cooler as Brandon shut the door behind them.

She opened the lid and began to remove the items one by one. “I got these for you,” Cassandra said as she removed a six pack of blonde ale. “You said you didn’t like IPAs, so I thought you could try these.” Brandon titled his head. It was not a brand he had heard of before. “And since I don’t actually like beer, I bought these,” she stated as she held up a six pack of apple cider. Cassandra placed them side by side on Brandon’s desk. “And because I was nervous about the bottles rattling when I walked down the hallway, I used these,” holding up a small stack of paper bags. Brandon chuckled. It was her attention to detail that he appreciated most.

They each popped open a bottle and clinked to a successful pre-mobilization. They settled in across from each other to begin their last conversation before the big event. As customary, work dominated the conversation, at least initially. Soon the dialog shifted and Brandon began to engage in a more personal manner. He started to tell Cassandra why he was the way that he was, and why certain things affected him in different ways.

She listened as he described his childhood and never being thought good enough by his parents. His experiences with home schooling did not aptly prepare him for his journey to public high school. He didn’t like to rely on other people because he didn’t want their good deeds to be used as leverage against him later. People’s selfishness and drama left him feeling depleted. He was running on empty and no one seemed to notice or care.

Cassandra’s face softened. “I care about you.”

"I know you do. Thank you," Brandon replied as he offered her a like-minded grin.

"Do *I* deplete you?" Cassandra asked tenderly. "You can be honest." She held her breath.

"Everyone does," Brandon answered as he exhaled and averted his gaze. "I'm an introvert, all interaction is draining." His eyes found hers. She hoped her interactions had not drained him. She didn't want to be one of those energy suckers he talked about.

Cassandra gazed out the window to regain her thoughts. "You know," she began slowly, "You and I are not that different." She watched Brandon's curiosity peak. "Our personalities are very similar, but for entirely different reasons."

Brandon listened as she recalled stories from her own childhood. No one seemed to notice her growing up. She achieved so people would see her. "It's like *what do I have to do to get some attention around here*?" His face softened as she spoke. A wave of familiarity washed over him. "That's why I'm constantly seeking validation. I don't know how to not do that. Even as a Christian, I can't stop." She was refreshingly human. To Brandon, that was her most admirable trait.

The one hour deadline was fast approaching, and Brandon's eyes followed hers to the clock. She waited for him to say something. Instead, he turned towards her and began to elaborate on his own relationships. She smiled. She knew his time was valuable, and she was beginning to see that maybe so was his time with her.

It was a gradual shift she had noticed with Brandon over the last month. Everything about the way he interacted with her seemed softer. The way he looked at her when she spoke to him. His level of comfort around her. The frequency he would embrace her head with his. The depth and sincerity behind his eyes as he absorbed her pain. His willingness to engage in activities inside her personal bubble.

But not everything he did was movie magic. Some of it was actually kind of disgusting, like belching, or farting, or having the bathroom door open just enough to leave little to the imagination. Some of it was just familiar, like sitting on the desk next to her while she typed, or leaning over her shoulder to see what she was looking at, or helping himself to objects within reach so he could inquire of their significance. Some of it promoted sexual chemistry, like having her examine his chest muscles to check for abnormalities, or squeezing her leg when he couldn't give her a hug, or changing his shirt right in front of her. Cassandra blushed when she imagined him bare chested. She didn't even get the full exposure and it still made her tingly with excitement.

Brandon shifted the conversation to her. "No offense, but your divorce nearly destroyed me." Fully grounded back in reality, Cassandra turned to him in surprise. "It was constant. I was barely hanging on." *Barely hanging on*? Cassandra knew she had barely escaped the divorce unscathed, but she never knew it had been so rough on Brandon. "I didn't even do anything and was still being dragged into the middle of it." Her heart softened and filled with regret. She never meant to hurt him. She hoped he knew that.

Her story had been part of a larger theme of how people equal drama. Brandon hated drama. She hoped he didn't hate her. "I'm sorry," she contended.

His eyes grew tender, "It's okay," he admitted. "Without drama there would be no life. If we didn't have drama, we would have nothing to talk about," he said as he flashed her a Brandon Fletcher original smile.

"I suppose," Cassandra admitted. She knew why the divorce had devastated her; she was emotionally invested. Did that mean Brandon was too? Even still, Cassandra still felt the need to defend herself. "I know it was a lot," she began, "but it was never my intent to steal your energy, even when I didn't have any. You re-charged my battery. Many times I had just enough left to interact with your energy and to bring both of our levels up. Our personalities complement each other, we each fill in the missing pieces pretty well." Brandon stared at her in affirmation and couldn't help but grin in her direction. She could tell he was pleased with her answer. He enjoyed working with her in every aspect and admired her appreciation of him.

Brandon caught sight of the clock. This time he *did* have to go. He stood up and pulled her firmly into him. He rested his head on hers, reflecting on an afternoon of familiar testimonies. With Brandon, Cassandra had made a habit of stating the obvious without expecting a response. "You mean a lot to me, just wanted you to know."

Thrown off by her wording, he asked quizzically, "What did you say?" Cassandra repeated her words. Brandon leaned into their hug and breathlessly uttered, "You mean a lot to me too." Cassandra's heart melted. Maybe he really did love her.

***

Dating. The final frontier. The last hurdle Cassandra needed to clear before she could get her life unstuck. She needed to date to meet people. She needed to date to develop her ability to relate to others. She needed to date to get over her relationship hang-ups. She needed to date to move past her hurts and get what she really wanted. She wanted Brandon. Cassandra wondered if dating other people would help her achieve that.

She didn't want to be one of those women who sat around waiting for Prince Charming to come riding on his horse, or riding on an airplane back from deployment. She needed to know she could find that feeling of safety and assuredness now, independent of any dream she might be seeking. What she wouldn't give to have someone in her arms at the end of a long day. Someone she could turn to when life knocked her to her knees. Someone who would stand up for her when David threatened to undo her. He was the other part of the equation. How would a relationship look with *him* in the picture?

During the pre-divorce train up, Cassandra sat in nervous desperation as she waited to see on which list she appeared. She had broken the news to David, and was waiting for him to determine which type of punishment she would receive for ruining his life, not to mention waiting on God to throw in whatever wrath He saw fit. She wanted to be strong and confident, but she was in no position to barter. She was the one who initiated the divorce. She would be lucky to even receive joint custody.

Cassandra's confidence ebbed and flowed in the months leading up until d-day. She would proceed with a lawyer. No she wouldn't. She would make a case against David citing his mental health and physical limitations as reasons he couldn't care for the kids. No she couldn't. She would highlight his lack of income and lack of means to support the children. Maybe she would. She was afraid of upsetting him and disrupting the co-parenting relationship. In the end, she conceded to half of all her financial assets, joint legal custody and a week on week off parenting arrangement. He had gotten almost exactly half of everything, yet it never seemed enough for him. He wanted her to suffer the way he had suffered. He wanted to constantly remind her of the mistakes she had made and that "bad" people didn't deserve mercy. He wanted her to know that she was unattractive and no one would want her. He wanted her to know that their children were a constant reminder of their failed marriage, and he would never stop resenting her every day for the rest of his life.

Cassandra didn't need constant reminders, she already knew. He had already told her, many times. She hadn't forgotten. Cassandra often felt like a puppy trying to please her owner; if she were loving and did just enough of the "right" thing, he would eventually see and stop punishing her. Although he never hit her, with every cutting comment she would cower. Every inflection, every accusation, and every cut on her character made her feel less than. Cassandra was only 4'11'' to begin with. Every unkind word and every unkind action cut her down inch by inch. If she had to assign a numeric value to her emotional stature, she would barely be twelve inches tall.

In the wake of the divorce Cassandra thought a relationship would be the perfect antidote to her pain. She was in pain because she was lonely. She was lonely because she wasn't in a loving relationship. She wasn't in a loving relationship because she was not with someone who could appreciate her as a person. If she found someone to love her, they would bring the joy she had been missing into her life. It seemed plausible. The only factor she hadn't considered was that maybe she didn't love herself.

She first got the idea from an email newsletter she had signed up to receive in the wake of the divorce. It boasted finding the ideal relationship and identified factors that often put Mr. or Mrs. Right on hold. This particular episode focused on anger and frustration. Cassandra's interest was sparked and she continued reading. Overly critical to others? *Yes.* Blames others for their actions? *Absolutely.* Thinking everyone had what they needed except for you? *Everyday.* Cassandra got to the punch line: *You likely don't love yourself.* She re-read the statement. Maybe she didn't love herself? *Impossible*. She had only wanted the best for herself.

Cassandra continued to see reminders of this message in emails, Facebook feeds, and church messages. She wondered if there was any truth in this statement. She was angry at others because she didn't love herself? Maybe people were just that annoying, she reasoned. She could see where she might have thought that for ordinary relationships like with her kids or her immediate family, but romantic relationships were a whole different category. They were something entirely different.

Cassandra continued to ponder this idea through her Thanksgiving food box prep, women's Bible study and miscellaneous shopping that weekend. God sought to reward her charitable acts of service with bonus babysitter time, so she took a detour to the book store. She loved all things academic. Being surrounded by books was like a marathon for her brain. If Cassandra's mind were a horse it would be at full gallop, running the expanse of store, wall to wall. Physically she felt a warm tingling in her heart and a cool rush of knowledge coursing through her veins. Mentally she felt the wheels of her brain kick into full gear. Emotionally her problems disappeared and her dreams were only limited to her wildest imagination. Here everything was possible. What Cassandra wouldn't give to be a full time resident of the possible.

National Novel Writing Month had drawn her to the *New Arrivals* and *Exceptional Value* sections of the book store. The shelves were bursting with new authors and Cassandra marveled at the amount of self-actualization that had to occur for people to get their books published and put on the shelf. *Don't Forget About Me!...* My *Better Self... If God Were Your Therapist...* Cassandra picked up the last book title and thumbed through it. 88 pages. It wasn't a novel. It wasn't even a full fledged self-help book. It was simply some thoughts on a paper arranged in a logical and comprehensive manner. She flipped the book over. $6.98. That was an exceptional value indeed. She picked up a daily devotional for moms and was on her way.

The book was an easy read and made her wonder why she invested in other people's anger. David had been the main energy sucker. True he was ill-tempered, manipulative and self-serving, but the power to overcome lay not in him changing his attitude or even Cassandra wishing magical thinking upon her situation, the solution lay within Cassandra herself. As long as her ego was getting something out of the exchange, her self-esteem wouldn't be able to rise and she would be critical of everyone and everything she encountered. The key was to let go. Simple, yet surprisingly complex.

How could she let go when David constantly drug her into his delusions? *Stop expecting a relationship with him.* Cassandra read that again. How could she stop expecting a relationship with him when he was the father of her children? It would seem that not all people in life warranted relationships. Furthermore some were not capable of having them. As long as expectations for that relationship still existed, frustration would abound every time. Cassandra paused as a light went off in her head. *Some people were not capable of relationships. David was not capable of relationships. I need to stop expecting one from him.*

Cassandra needed to give up the dream of mending the relationship with David because there wasn't one to mend. She needed to let go of her expectations and simply let him exist. He lived in his world and she lived in hers. The children were travelers between the two. His opinions had no bearing on her ability to co-parent, just as hers had no bearing on his. She was not to blame every time the kids said or did something that he didn't like. They were their own people with their own personalities. She couldn't control them any more than she could control him. In the same manner he had no ability to control her. She was in charge of where her life would go and when. He could not direct her life choices. Not anymore.

David didn't like what she was doing so he would lash out. He wanted to control her actions and twisted her thoughts and feelings to make her feel guilty. He didn't care about anything she did until it affected him directly. The children were his excuse to reeling her back in. If Cassandra were honest with herself, her marriage had been no different. He engaged in these behaviors when they were "happily married." What incentive would he have to act any differently now that their union was legally dissolved? She concluded David had always been the person that he was now, and the only difference was he was no longer legally or morally obligated to try to control his impulses.

Cassandra settled in on the couch with a cup of hot chocolate and reengaged her original premise; the decision to date. What did she expect to gain from the experience? Did she actually want to date, or did she just want to be intimate with someone? Was she looking for a forever boyfriend, or simply someone to pass the time with until Brandon came back? What did she anticipate happening when he *did* come back?

That he would throw his arms around her and tell her he was now ready to engage in whatever kind of relationship she wanted? *Yes*, yes she did.

Her first two internet stints ultimately led her to find her respective husbands. She had tried a speed dating event recently, and left with zero phone numbers and an equal number of prospects. In the months following her dissolution, she learned of a few inquiries of her relationship status at work, and was later informed that two non-commissioned officers asked for her phone number. To her knowledge, neither of them had received the requested information. She didn't even know who they were. She looked at some singles events, but nothing seemed conducive to her childcare schedule. Her boxing class was 99.5% female. Maybe online *was* the best option.

Cassandra perused the interwebs to find the most effective online bargaining chip. There was no shortage of reviews. *Plenty of Fish* promised just that, both good and bad, chum and premiere fillet. *Ok Cupid* seemed to come highly rated. *It's Just Lunch* came with professional matchmaking services and a price tag to match. *Match* was tried and true. New editions like *Bumble* were up and coming. *Tinder* was known for its famous s*wipe left* feature. Cassandra hovered over *Hinge*, the application that was designed to be deleted. Interesting. It seemed low pressure and casual, and subscribers could even post "deal breakers." She would go with that one.

The profile required five pictures. Cassandra didn't know if she even had that many on her phone. There were plenty of her children, posing in various configurations. There were pictures of medicine bottles and parenting calendars. The selfie department was running a little low. She would need to hunt down a few more. She wondered if her phone had a timer. Nothing outdated. No bad angles or blurred faces, she was trying to create the most current and complete picture as possible.

She scrolled through her phone. The kids' first boat ride. Cute, but not quite what she was going for. Her Florida visit with Tommy, that might work. Her half-marathon picture with finisher medal. Sure, guys liked a winner. Her dining out picture with Brandon. Cassandra's thumb hovered over the image. They were both in their fancy military uniforms. Men always loved a woman in uniform. But did they love them with their arms around someone else she wondered? Brandon had helped her with many things the last couple of years, maybe helping her find a guy was something he would be able to add to his list of accomplishments. She hesitated. It was a good picture, but she continued her search. Brandon could save up his good will for another day.

Next, she would need to talk about herself, but not too much. Less than 30 words, three times. There really wasn't a place to talk about yourself per say, just a place to list your top three conversation prompts. If you were creative, you could sneak a description into your answer. Otherwise, the pictures would speak for themselves. If a member found you interesting, they could click on a heart and send you a like. If you went above and beyond to upgrade to the Premiere Membership, you could have unlimited access to email communication. For $11.95 a month it was tempting, but Cassandra opted to stick with the baseline plan. She was eager to get to *the app that was designed to be deleted* portion of the application. Upgrading might slow her down. The website used its intuitive abilities to make the upgrade for her free of charge. *How kind*, she thought, or *how smart*. Either way, she was determined to utilize the website to its fullest extent.

Things started off with a bang and Cassandra was getting likes right and left. From cute guys too, and young. Like super young. Like men in their early twenties, who lived on the other side of the country. She exchanged email banter with a sporty guy that went to one of the churches in her area. Another guy called her *beautiful* and asked what she was up to. Cassandra was enjoying the attention. Interest from her male fan club persisted for a single day. It would seem the trade off for *preferences* and *deal breakers* was a limited selection of male admirers. One such *male* prospect used to be female but was now seeking women to have and to hold. A click of the mouse and her worries were gone.

Cassandra had kids and needed someone open to having them. She wanted someone who wasn't afraid to express their faith. Smoking cigarettes or any other substance was a no no. Drinking was okay socially. They would need to have a job, anything that paid and that showed promise for advancement. They would need to be attractive. Cassandra's definition of attractive was constantly evolving, but there had to be a physical spark when she saw their picture. If not, the big black X was their fate.

By no means did Cassandra think she was searching for the perfect man. She knew he didn't exist. She also knew that she was tired of "close enough," and that is what prompted her to marry two people she had no business ending up with. It was like the house she rented after the divorce was finalized; it wasn't perfect, but she could see herself and the kids living comfortably there. The floor plan was open. There were no stairs. The landscape was conducive to small children, plus boasted multiple parks within walking distance. Cassandra was willing to put up with the slightly uneven floors and 70's style décor in the name of comfort. That's how she felt about her men too.

Cassandra's thoughts naturally shifted to Brandon. He was grumpy, had a jaded view of the world, bit his nails and chewing tobacco was one of his daily pastimes. Still Cassandra loved him with all of her heart. Being with him made her feel alive. She felt listened to. He validated her feelings. He gave his time and attention to her when he didn't have any. He gave of himself everything he was capable of giving. He didn't always agree with her, but would seek to understand her point of view. He never intentionally hurt her and genuinely enjoyed spending time with her. In his own way he loved her too, and that was more than anyone else had ever given her. More than that, he filled her needs exactly the way he was. There were no gaps or shortages. Just a fulfillment knowing that he truly loved and cared for her, even if he couldn't bring himself to say it out loud.

He had been hurt. He had a series of unfortunate relationships, and it was two broken people trying to help each other put the pieces back together. He was real. He was honest. He was genuine, and Brandon often said the same about her. He didn't like to be touched but he hugged her because he knew she enjoyed it. More than paying lip service to the gesture, he hugged her with his whole body. He conveyed meaning in everything he did. He had even let her hold his hand and kiss him. He feared intimacy but had let her in. Cassandra wondered if she would ever find someone like Brandon. She wondered if she should even bother. He was perfect, and everyone else fell short in Cassandra's eyes.

***

California was everything she imagined it to be. In fact, not much had changed since she had been there one year ago. It wasn't quite as hot, the air was a bit cleaner, yet it still reeked of sweat and misery. She should get an Army Commendation Medal for coming back to this place a second time. The mission was much more simplified than last year, but was proving to be more complex than their brigade resupply mission had ever been. All they had to do was support the mobilizing Soldiers. That was it. Cassandra was in charge of that operation, except that she wasn't, well...kind of. She was in charge of her people. Someone else was in charge of the other people. Someone entirely different was in charge of both of them. The only issue was Cassandra outranked them all. She wondered in what world a Captain outranked a Major.

The bus ride down was long, hot and miserable, leaving Cassandra weighing the benefits of convoying. She arrived at o'dark hundred that muggy September morning. Deployment eve was here, and she stood at the threshold. The inevitable was finally here. She stepped off the bus into the unknown.

The whole thing had been her plan from the start. It was her coordination with the other units to ensure their efforts were fully aligned. It was her desire to take as much off of the deploying Soldiers plates as she could. It was a labor of love really, and everything she did she did with the intent to make *his* life easier. He had done so much for her, the least she could do was give him all of her final efforts. This deployment Cassandra would lose the ability to affect Brandon's life on any large scale. All she had was the present.

Cassandra started with a basic premise; Brandon was deploying. Because he was deploying, his time would be spent completing tasks required of him to leave the country. Because he was busy completing pre-mobilization tasks, he likely wouldn't have an abundance of time to spend with her. Since his time would be in short supply, Cassandra needed to make sure it was as stress free as possible. Anything she could effect, she would. She would do it for him knowing that he wouldn't have that continued support once he left the country.

Ammunition, fuel, medical support, maintenance and recovery; it was all up for bid. Her support operations cell even expanded to include range operations. The Task Force would get the royal treatment. By proxy, Brandon and his company would receive the same level of care. Brandon was a well intentioned logistician and did not do chaos. Poor planning and sloppy execution were his arch nemesis, and Cassandra felt much the same way. She recalled the chaos that ensued last summer despite their well thought out courses of action. The plan was solid, it was the people that got in the way. Rather, people thinking it would be more conducive to not follow a plan that was the issue. Cassandra had helped Brandon sort out the chaos last year, and she would help him again this year. She would do her hest to give him a smooth send off.

Despite her clear intentions, the lines of communication were anything but. Plans were laid out from start to finish. Yet it was as if someone decided to turn her logistical blueprint sideways, tear off of a corner and scribble on it with a crayon. Unsuspecting passersby would see the patched together picture and conclude the plan was ready to go. Cassandra couldn't believe how this training was playing out. She watched in dismay as lines of communication broke down from one person to another. The telephone game ran rampant, despite often being in the same room. She was used to dealing with suck, but this training was almost too much. Her only saving grace was that she wasn't alone in her thinking.

Cassandra's phone rang and despite the familiar name scrolling across the screen, she answered, "This is Major Miller."

"Good morning Ma'am. This is Lieutenant Roberts. You are on speaker phone with Captain Fletcher. We were wondering if you could help us."

This was a daily occurrence since arriving in California. Every day was something new. Some days were so ridiculous that she considered changing her greeting to *Crisis hotline, this is Major Miller, how can I help you*? The day was still relatively new, and Lieutenant Roberts was her first call. Lucky for him he got all of the pep and cheer that end of the day patrons often missed.

"The water buffalo? Yeah, I think we can help you out with that," Cassandra contended.

An enthusiastic "Thanks Ma'am!" echoed in her ear.

"No problem. Hope you guys enjoy the rest of your day," she stated as she ended the call. Cassandra enjoyed exchanging pleasantries. They gave her a sense of normalcy. It was hot. It was gross. It was California. She often pretended they had all booked a hellacious vacation with the same subpar travel agent, and California was just a brief stop before they reached their lush vacation destination. Cassandra sighed. This would be the first of many calls she would receive. They liked to take turns. The next one would be Sergeant Andrews. Captain Fletcher would call every now and again just to shake things up. Those were her favorite, although she could do without the speaker phone.

Still, it was Brandon and he was her favorite customer. That's probably why he called her. Despite the obvious, Cassandra took solace in the fact that he *chose* to call her. It meant that he trusted her and thought of her highly enough to be able to solve his problems. She was glad she could be a sounding board for him, and since she was in the problem solving business, she wondered if there were any other items she could assist him with. She was a relationships expert, and would be happy to offer following on training.

The training went; forward, backwards, sideways and in a circle back to where it started again. That type of organization drove Cassandra up the wall. It was like she was running very slowly in quicksand. Whenever she felt like she was gaining some traction, someone around her would panic and flail their arms about, dragging her down with the weight of their problems. Yet she was not without the weight of her own problems. Cassandra was still struggling with the aftermath of her divorce, and imagined her battery to be at about 50 percent. Then there was David. He had the kids for her three week sentence in California. The only thing that had changed since last year was they were no longer married. In David's eyes, she was in California, pining after some guy that wasn't him and he was stuck watching their children, again.

Just the mention of a return trip to California sent him into fits of rage, only he pretended they were moral acts of parental concern. The children would miss her, he would say. She had an obligation to find local healthcare for them before she went. He would need more child support he contended. After all he would be taking them for more than his "fair turn," and she needed to reimburse him for his time and expenses. He wanted her to have control over nothing, but gave her free reign to make all the decisions then resented her for it. He wasn't the only one that wished she would have deployed to Kosovo. Cassandra would have welcomed a year-long deployment with brigade headquarters as a chance to regroup and regain her sanity. A year without David would have been a blessing. But here she was, the lead actress in *As Cassandra's World Turns, Volume II.*

Cassandra made her expectations clear before departing. She would welcome pictures of the kids, she would even welcome texts to ask when would be a good time to talk to the children. What she would not welcome was text messages for any other purpose, especially text messages to vent. His concerns were no longer her concerns; she had a job to do and didn't want to be distracted. Week one passed with a single call to David. The kids were doing well. Hunter got some new dinosaurs, or maybe it was pajamas. He was four, it was hard to tell. Heather babbled excitedly into the phone before wandering off, and she didn't even have to talk to David. All seemed well.

Week two yielded more of the same. Cassandra couldn't believe her luck. Maybe this would be the first training event she would make it through where she wasn't harassed by her kids' father. Two days into week three and communication began to break down. Much like during their marriage, two weeks was the maximum threshold for change. The instigation started with a seed. Were her monthly drills in town or out of town the rest of the calendar year? Cassandra hesitated. She knew David well enough to know he wouldn't stop there. Why hadn't she brought enough diapers to daycare to sustain the kids through the duration of her training? He wasn't even there and the mere idea of him existing on the other end of the phone was beginning to repulse her.

Back in the war torn fields of California, ranges and ammunition distribution emerged as the next hot button issues. Cassandra was coming to the end of her tour and her patience was wearing thin. She was over it. She was over the training and the ridiculousness of the mission. She was over trying to fix everyone else's mistakes. She was over David in his entirety. She had had enough, and his text messages had been the final straw.

Why didn't he get more child support he wondered? Because he was already being overpaid since he got credit for exactly half of the year and had the children far less than that. He could have them for the rest of month and still not even come to half the amount of time she had them. Why didn't she bring diapers to daycare? She already had. She didn't know it was her job from now until the end of time to always supply essentials for the kids. Why did he have to watch the kids when she was in town for drill? Because the divorce decree said so, in town or not had no bearing on the court ruling. He wanted to go hunting on his parenting week and she would need to watch the kids. The parenting plan specified right of first refusal. He asked, she said no. It was as simple as that.

In that conversation, Cassandra also learned she was a lying adulteress who couldn't be trusted. Her family was lazy and viewed him as the bad guy. The less time the kids spent with her the better. Cassandra was waiting for the mobile app that allowed her to strangle someone through the phone. She didn't hate a lot of people, but she hated him. He could fall of the edge of the earth that night and the only tears she would shed would be for the children growing up without a father. If only it was day two of a three day cancer, then maybe she could show some forgiveness.

Cassandra blocked his number for the rest of the night. She ran six miles to take the edge off, and after she was done, called her best friend to get a grown up's perspective on things. Tommy agreed the cancer would have been the ideal situation. And although she couldn't control David's responses, she could still control her own. She didn't have to be talked to that way. He didn't own her. She could be happy despite his grumpiness. If she were being honest with herself, Cassandra had condoned that most of her marriage.

With her temperature now within the acceptable range, she shifted her thoughts to something more pleasant. There was something inspiring, almost magical about the night sky. She recalled the year before on their extended military sponsored camping trip and how Brandon had spent many a night talking her off the cliff. She had done the same for him. They liked to switch. It kept things interesting. Maybe they would have a chance to talk before she left. He wasn't even gone yet and she already missed him. She needed him to hold her hand if she expected to make it through training unscathed.

The universe must have sensed the collective suffering floating about the warm southern air, and sought the need to bring Cassandra and Brandon together whenever the situation allowed. She ran into him often in the dining facility. It seemed like she saw him there at least once a day. If it wasn't him it was one of his lieutenants. They were close enough to speak for him, it was almost like having him there. He had stopped by to see her on occasion at her support cell operations center. She even went to visit his company headquarters, "coincidentally" ending her evening runs on his barracks block. They talked almost every day on the phone, and texting abounded with every major maneuver. It was all work centered, but it brought her to Brandon. And he after all, was her primary objective.

Cassandra complained of the collective suck but secretly didn't want it to end. Every day was like a year. But every day brought her closer to saying goodbye to Brandon, this time for real. She would even be leaving four days before him, but was thankful her unique overlap shift gave her more time to spend with her friend. It was almost worth the extended tongue lashings from David. Saying good-bye though was almost more bittersweet than having already said her peace and have him walk away. Each passing day was a gift, though was one day closer to the inevitable. She had prepped a year for this moment, and the deployment wasn't unlike any other training event she had prepared for, only this time she would need to do it without her friend by her side.

As far as goodbyes go, Cassandra was granted quite a few of them, much more than she had originally set out for. In her mind, she was expecting a single epic event, complete with hugging, kissing and all of the sentimental discourse one might expect to hear at a final departure. Instead what she had found was a series of small interconnected events that allowed her to build on her previous encounter, and that allowed her to express her sentiment in chunks. Brandon's sentimentality meter was a bit touchy, and it didn't take much to push his needle into the red. Cassandra was sure Brandon preferred his sentimentality in bite sized pieces. That was probably why he had granted her so many good-bye occasions.

She struggled with wanting to tell him she loved him and that she would be waiting for him when he got back. She wanted to be the encouraging person he needed her to be and support Team Fletcher. She wondered if divulging her feelings would help him feel more encouraged on his journey or hinder his thoughts. But really how could he *not* know that she felt that way? Cassandra had given him all of the clues. What's more, she said *I love you* often in an effort to take the sting out of it. He knew she loved him. The big question in Cassandra's mind was if he loved her that way too.

They had both founded the *Miller-Fletcher Center for Logistical Excellence*, and had the t-shirt to prove it. Along with her son Hunter, Cassandra and Brandon had both been characters in a hard bound book she designed just for him. *The Adventures of Brandon and Cassandra* was hardly a best seller, but was a compelling reminder of the friendship they shared and the bond that they forged.

Cassandra told him once that she wanted him to keep her apprised of his future plans because she wanted to be part of them. As she rebounded from the weight of her own words, she stared in disbelief as Brandon side-stepped her statement. She initially felt brave for even venturing to text it to him. She chickened out on her in person opportunity, blaming his eyes as her reason for self-doubt. They undid her every time. Cassandra summoned the courage to repeat her statement. This time she got a little more traction. Even still, he would let her know as soon as he knew; ambiguous, but still encouraging. Ambiguity and encouragement were hallmark Brandon Fletcher friendship traits. If anything, at least he was consistent.

It was her final night at the training site and Cassandra felt like a balloon that had been deflated. Part of her wanted to seek Brandon out for one final rendezvous in the hopes that he could re-inflate her spirits. Another part of her wanted to blow away across the cool September sky and never think of this terrible place again. On her way back to the barracks, Cassandra was intercepted by Sergeant First Class Keaton. She knew her two last names ago, and had met Cassandra when Cassandra was in the unit the first time. They exchanged mission related woes and pent up frustrations. Cassandra took solace in sharing her burdens with someone who understood the stupidity and futility of poor planning. After an hour, Cassandra was good. She was ready to go to bed and dream about better things.

Scarcely more than a hundred meters into her plan, she was intercepted outside of her barracks door by Chief Paulson. He wanted to know if she liked beer because he was planning on having a get together in the maintenance bay after hours. Cassandra looked at him quizzically, wondering if he knew he was discussing alcohol with a field grade officer. "No I don't like beer," Cassandra stated flatly. "But if you are having them, then yes I will have one."

Chief Paulson lowered his voice and leaned in, "Well if you don't like beer then what *do* you like?"

"Anything that doesn't taste like alcohol," Cassandra responded in the same hushed tone. "Do you want some money?"

"You're good. We'll come pick you up after we run to the store," he affirmed.

Cassandra counted the offenses. She was up to three. Chief Paulson was going to retrieve alcohol in a government vehicle. The list of offenses grew to four.

She didn't know about anyone else's pre-deployment experience, but this was definitely one for the books. Cassandra couldn't recall the last time training was so disorganized, no wait, yes she could; last year in California, April at the coast, the April before that in Washington. So maybe it happened all of the time. Maybe that's what her unit did was mess things up. Only this time, the messing up was entirely the result of someone else's hand.

True to his word, Chief Paulson picked Cassandra up within the hour and headed towards the unauthorized. Cassandra was the officer in charge for this mission but would authorize the evening's misconduct. She was already preparing her sworn statement when they pulled up to the outline of the dilapidated building. As Chief Paulson pulled back the barn style door, Cassandra considered that she hadn't even met the mechanics yet. She could recognize their names on paper, but she couldn't put a face to a name. In the moment she ventured from the California dusk into the bright lights of the bay, she wondered if it was okay that she came. Aside from the Warrant Officer that had invited her, the crowd consisted of four junior enlisted Soldiers and one Staff Sergeant. A look of momentary surprise took hold of one of the junior enlisted, before responding, "Hello Ma'am."

A series of folding chairs sat around a blue outdoor cooler and a Mike's Hard Lemonade made its way into Cassandra's hand. She took a drink and settled into a chair as her audience began to relax. Beverages flowed from the cooler in both directions. Soon music ensued, and Chief Paulson took musical requests. Breakdancing and rapping broke out across the concrete floor. Cassandra couldn't remember the last time she laughed so hard. Chief Paulson raised a bottle, "To a great AT!" That evening had clearly been her best one the entire training. There might not have been much to toast, but at least it would end on a high note. The only thing that would have made the evening better was if Brandon were there to share it with her.

Three drinks in, she asked Chief Paulson if he could keep a secret. After confiding her interest in Captain Fletcher to him, he confided something to her; he was getting divorced, for the second time. He solicited her ear because her former Battalion Commander thought she might have some insight. Cassandra thought that was an odd thing to boast, but there she was. If he wanted to talk she would listen.

His story was not unlike her own, except that there had been no hostility just "growing apart." They had a son together. They shared financial assets. She did not approve of his military life and felt stifled. Cassandra could relate. What was he supposed to do? All Cassandra could do was listen as he bared his soul.

She couldn't believe he seemed so put together. He was so confident, and even bordered unapproachable and critical at times. Who knew he was secretly falling apart inside? He was a braver soul than she and his optimism astounded her. His belief that it would all work out drove every action. How he managed to find the energy to come to work and fix the battalion's maintenance issues were beyond Cassandra. In that moment she appreciated his vulnerability.

He seemed to have sensed her own vulnerability and asked if she had thought to invite Captain Fletcher. Cassandra shook her head. "I told him I was coming here, but I didn't ask if he wanted to come," she paused. "He never wants to come to things like this."

Chief Paulson studied her face before concluding, "I bet I can get him to come here."

Cassandra's eyes were wide with amazement. "It's ten o'clock at night!" she exclaimed.

"You don't believe me, do you? He and I are friends too. I bet you I can get him to come here. Wanna bet?" he asked as he stretched out his hand.

Cassandra took his hand. "Yes, I will take that bet."

Chief Paulson pushed his chair back and stepped outside. Moments later he returned with phone in hand. He put his hand on Private Smith's shoulder and said, "Hey, call Corporal Tyson and tell him after he gets done dropping those guys off to swing by building 4021 to pick up Captain Fletcher." Private Smith handed him the phone. "Building 4021. Yeah, Captain Fletcher…he will be waiting outside." He hung up the phone and sank back into his seat. Cassandra stared in amazement. Partly because she had last track of the offenses, and partly out of sheer morbid curiosity of how Chief Paulson had hoodwinked him into coming at such a late hour.

"I told you I would get him to come," he said with a smirk.

All Cassandra could do was stare until she finally managed, "How did you get him to say yes?"

"I just told him I needed to talk to him. I told him I had something to say to him." He could sense Cassandra's skepticism. "I told you we were friends."

Twenty minutes later the barn door opened and in walked Captain Fletcher. Cassandra let out a sharp inhalation. He was still in his uniform, but there he was, just as predicted. Upon seeing her, Brandon too inhaled sharply before averting his gaze. He sat in an open chair as Chief Paulson handed him a Mike's Lemonade. Brandon placed it unopened on the floor and gave him a tilted stare. It was obvious to Cassandra that he thought he was being set up. Brandon and Chief locked eyes and it was apparent to her that they in fact were friends. A fondness washed over Brandon's face, and Cassandra listened in amazement to tales of previous deployments and how Brandon had been there for Chief during his stroke. No wonder why he came tonight, she thought. Brandon genuinely cared about his well-being and they had a history together.

Cassandra peaked at her watch. It was now eleven thirty. She turned her watch to Chief Paulson and stated through pursued lips, "I'm running out of time."

Chief turned to Brandon and posed, "It's getting late, do you want to walk her back?"

His words hung in the air like a pungent spray. "*Walk her back*?" Brandon retorted. "That's like a mile!"

Cassandra let the weight of her embarrassment wash over her. Chief tried again. "Do you want us to take you back?"

"Yeah, it's getting late and I've got a lot to do tomorrow."

Cassandra chimed in, "I'll go back too." As far as she could recount, offenses were now at seven. Surely adding fraternization would be the least of her concerns.

She settled into the front seat of the truck as Brandon settled in behind her. She looked across at her driver. "Are you sure you are able to drive?"

"Oh, I'm good. I actually drive better when I'm…"

"Let's not finish that sentence. Do me a favor and put on your seat belt though." Cassandra could see the headlines all over the *Army Times*, at least a seatbelt would be one less offense. It was less than a mile and mostly flat, chances were high they would survive any potential rollover. Hopefully it wouldn't come to that. But if it did, at least her final moments would have been spent with Brandon.

The truck pulled around Brandon's block, "Just let me out here and I'll walk." They came to a stop and Cassandra hopped out too.

She turned towards her driver, "Don't go anywhere I'll be right back."

In the ambiance of the headlights, Cassandra met Brandon for one last embrace. Contrary to his Army demeanor, he met her embrace with equal tenderness as he rested his head on hers and pulled her in close. She tried a few times during training to offer him hugs, but was met with an uncomfortable stiffness each time. He didn't want anyone to get the wrong perception. But here in the dark, on her final night, he consented to her emotional sentiment. "I'll miss you," she breathed into his chest.

Like he was gasping for air, Brandon repeated back to her, "I'll miss you too." They lingered a little longer before Cassandra headed back to her side of the post.

Once inside, she tiptoed across the squeaky barracks floor into the bathroom, chuckling under her breath. She felt like a school girl coming home after curfew, trying not to wake her parents. Cassandra never had a curfew because she had never actually been allowed to go out. Still, she imagined how the thrill of sneaking back in must have felt. From the shower bench she contemplated Brandon in all of his ambiguous splendor. Training had sucked, but she was glad she at least got to share in it with him. She wondered if he was still awake. After five drinks, she was finally thinking clearly and pulled out her phone.

She began, *I love you with all of my heart. I will miss you when you go. Take care of yourself and be safe.* Cassandra hit send. A minute later her phone let out a familiar *ding,* and her heart warmed at his response. *I love you too. Take care yourself, and thanks again for all of your help*. He even included a kissy face. Normally Cassandra would be inclined to think it was the drinks talking, but he didn't have any. He loved her too. She let those words wash over her like a warm spring rain. *I love you too*. Cassandra had ached to hear those words, and now finally had. She had been waiting this whole time to earn his affections, maybe Brandon was right and had shown her through his actions. Maybe this deployment eve was the catalyst he needed to finally express it out loud.

***

It was December 5th and the 30 day challenge had come and gone. By midnight on November 30th Cassandra had reached 32,000 words. It wasn't the 50,000 that the challenge warranted, nor was it where Cassandra wished to leave the story. Writing had become part of her daily battle rhythm and it was like a labor of love for her. It was her way of communing with Brandon when he was halfway across the world. She would finish because she owed it to him. December 18th would be her new mark on the wall. It allowed her to reach her objective at a comfortable pace without the distractions of the holidays encroaching. There was only one problem; she was almost out of things to write about.

The story largely related Cassandra's life over the past two years, and Brandon had been a big part of it. But he was deployed now, and without him to generate new tales of interest, she would be forced to make up her own narrative. Cassandra's anxiety began to rise. She wrote about Brandon because it was *easy*. Sure she spent many a night racking her brain over interesting facts and anecdotes to relate, but at the end of the day everything she wrote was grounded in truth. Making up stories was not one of her super powers. She wondered if she had 18,000 words worth of creativity left inside of her.

Hadn't the whole experience been an act of creativity though, she wondered? Didn't it take creativity to arrange the stories in a sequential fashion and choose which aspects to highlight? Didn't it take creativity to go back through items that were true and put a personal spin on them to connect the story to its readers? Didn't it take creativity to talk about complex feelings in a way that other people could understand and relate to? Cassandra pressed on with her story but felt like a fake.

It was just like her job. As the Support Operations Officer, her job was to support their brigade with logistical support like transportation, maintenance, medical, ammunition, fuel, food, water and automation support. Initially she thought the job too big for her, and even though it was her dream job, she had big shoes to fill. Her highly acclaimed predecessor would become her supervisor. Although she was a logistics officer, Cassandra often felt she knew very little about logistics. A real logistician could give text book answers of supply point distribution and forward logistics elements, and often waited for applause as they entered the room. Everything she learned she learned through observation and doing what made sense. Cassandra didn't wait for anyone's applause; she was too busy trying to fix everyone's logistical shortfalls so one would find out that she didn't actually have the skills to do her job.

She later learned some doctrinal terms for the practices she was already doing. No one had told her to do them, she just did them because they made sense. Finding holes in other people's plans was her specialty, as well as finding out who she could call to help dig her out of the logistical snares she often found herself in. Cassandra had attended a conference a few months back and everyone was asked to discuss an area of expertise. She racked her brain before determining her area of expertise was finding everyone else's area of expertise. It wasn't a copout, it was the truth. Everything she did depended on previously built relationships. Without them, Cassandra lacked the knowledge to get from point A to point B. She was largely successful because of others, and Brandon had always ensured her success.

Maybe that's why she missed him so much. More than just the warm and fuzzy feeling she got when he was around, he made her feel whole, both personally and professionally. He filled in the gaps that she herself couldn't fill, and she often did the same for him. He believed in her as a person and as a logistician. Without him there, who would cheer her on? Just like the theme of her life the past year, she wondered if cheering was a task she needed to undertake herself.

Be her own cheerleader? Cassandra didn't know the first thing about organized sports. It was so contrary to the way her life had been up until this point, she wasn't even sure how to conjure up such things. What did advocating for yourself *actually* look like, Cassandra contemplated. She wondered if it involved repeating affirming mantras to herself over and over until she believed them. Maybe she needed to look at life in a happy, more positive way so magically all of her problems would disappear. Perhaps it meant making amends with all of the people that had offended her. Did she have to abandon others needs and only focus on herself? Maybe it was learning to see life from a new perspective. Cassandra's last thought seemed the most probable, but how would she find that new perspective?

Maybe it was hiding under one of the bags in her boxing class. Perhaps it existed within the pages of her newly formed manuscript, or maybe it was resting between the seat cushions at church. It might be in the bowl of leftover Halloween candy, or perhaps at the finish line of her last race. Maybe it coursed through the stream at the park, or lie within her co-workers through collaboration on a new project. Introspection was a lot of work. Cassandra needed a break.

She got up to use the restroom and caught a glimpse of herself in the mirror. Her *Center for Logistical Excellence* t-shirt hung a little looser around her torso than it usually did. She contended it was stretched out and could benefit from a load of laundry. To confirm her theory, Cassandra raised the bottom edge of her shirt and examined the lower half of her torso. She twisted right to left and back again. A slanted line shown through her loose C-section skin, and a four pack of defined muscle threatened to upset perma-fat deposited just below the surface. She flexed her arm as the skin along her biceps tightened and formed a small bulge.

Cassandra changed into her pajama pants and watched as they fell loosely from her waist. Instead of clinging to her areas of most embarrassment, her medium sized shirt flowed freely over her mid-section. Cassandra turned sideways in the mirror again, this time to the opposite side. It seemed that both sides of her torso had been worked out evenly. She flexed her leg and ran her hands along the natural curve of her legs and butt. A pinch of fat was all she was able to muster. Cassandra stared quizzically in the mirror. Maybe the boxing class really was paying off.

She opened her laptop and scanned her word count; 900 words to go. She closed her eyes and focused her thoughts. The contest was over, no one was judging her. Cassandra breathed an audible sigh. She still wasn't sure where she was going, but she knew she would get there, eventually. Her fingers began to dance across the keys, faster and faster they worked in a rhythmic harmony. The train had left the station and began to navigate its way through the landscape of her mind. It followed her through twists, turns and through busy intersections. The train began to gradually slow before finally coming to a stop. Cassandra looked down at the bottom of the page; 3,000 words. Brandon wasn't mentioned, not even once.

Some days she didn't write at all, while others she wrote for hours. She wrote whenever the mood struck her, and with small children, sometimes she had to be selective about when the mood struck. Little people often opposed adult creativity during the daytime hours, and if she waited until they went to bed to put her thoughts to paper, she was often too tired and fuzzy headed to think. She quickly learned to maximize time without the kids. Other days she took advantage of a slow work week. Little by little Cassandra chipped away at her 50,000 word goal. She would make it. Her story would be heard.

The story helped her process her unresolved feelings and helped bring perspective to her experiences. It helped her see the love others were giving her despite her unwillingness to receive it. It gave Cassandra the escape she craved, with the added bonus of doing something to better her life. She wasn't just writing the book to pass the time, she wrote with the idea that it would somehow transform her life. She needed to get unstuck. Writing helped free her thoughts and focused her energies. She frequently left her writing sessions with a clearer sense of who she was and where she was going. Fear was often a companion on many of Cassandra's adventures. Fear could be in her book, but just couldn't be the main character, at least not anymore.

The alarm on Cassandra's phone dinged. She set her story aside and opened up her web browser. It was the first week of December. If she wanted a good deal she needed to act fast. She wondered why plane tickets were so expensive, and wondered since when two year olds had to start buying their own tickets. She had been saving for months, but she supposed it was just money. Cassandra sighed. With three clicks of the mouse tickets flooded her inbox. Now all she had to do was make it the airport with two toddlers. This would be her most daunting task yet. It would be worth extra points, and would make sure her supervisor included it on her next officer evaluation report.

***

D-Day had arrived. There would be traffic, she would need to find parking, and of course she would need to get there early to get a seat to the already overbooked venue. An hour and a half early should suffice. Cassandra stared out the window. Her buffer was slipping away. She hoped she would get there soon.

A white SUV slowly came to stop in front of her house and a young girl with long brown hair hopped out and started up the driveway. When she booked 8:30, the agency meant 8:30. Cassandra wrapped herself up in her tapered blue coat. She liked the way he looked at her when she wore it. Today would be her last chance to see that grin.

Hunter ran to open the door as Cassandra greeted her visitor with purse in hand. “You must be Jessica. This is Hunter, and this is his sister Heather.”

Jessica found herself being escorted down the hallway by two miniature sets of hands as Cassandra oriented her to the kids’ room and pantry. She briefed nap time and disclosed the location of nearby parks. She showed Jessica how to work the DVD player and was halfway out the door when she asked if there were any questions. Cassandra gave Hunter and Heather a hug and closed the door.

Cassandra paid the parking fee and proceeded to Exhibit Hall C in record time. The parking lot seemed rather empty for the amount of people that were anticipated, but perhaps she had beaten the crowds after all. She peered into the windows and saw tiny dancers prance the length of the hall. She found a quilting expo in Exhibit Halls A and B. As if she had somehow missed the event the first time, she looped around to recheck the buildings. Sure enough, no mobilization ceremony.

Cassandra pulled out her phone to check the location. Maybe she had the building number wrong, or maybe the time had changed. She read the words: *Convention Center.* She nodded her head. She was at the Convention Center. It was the same place she would be picking up her race packet the following weekend. *The Convention Center...* Cassandra mulled over the words in her head.

The mobilization ceremony was at the Convention Center. As if for the first time, she turned to the neon sign outside the exhibition hall and read the words out loud. She was at the *Expo Center*. A wave of panic washed over her. How far away was the Convention Center? Would she make it? What was the parking like? Would she be able to even get a seat? Cassandra turned her watch towards her. It was 9:10. The ceremony started at 10:00. She ran across the parking lot as fast as her heeled shoes would carry her and hopped in her truck. She hoped she was not too late.

The Convention Center wasn't as far away as she had imagined and it was 9:30 when she arrived at the venue. She waited her turn to hand over her second parking fee of the morning. She followed the line of cars, as her anxiety began to build regarding where she could park her monster truck. The fourth floor seemed safe, and despite its apparent proximity to the main floor, offered many worry free possibilities for Cassandra.

Cassandra followed a crowd of people to Exhibit Hall C. She grabbed a program and entered the room. It was 9:45 and seemingly plenty of seating. Cassandra didn't know why she had been so worried. She meandered her way through the crowd of Soldiers milling about on the drill floor. She recognized some, but Brandon was not among them. She made her way up to an apparent empty seat. Nope. It was taken, and so was the row behind it, and the three rows behind that one. People were blocking out seating by the dozen. All she needed was one seat. She petitioned a quiet Asian woman with her arms crossed. She nodded. Yes, Cassandra could sit there.

She settled into her seat as she breathed a sigh of relief. Moments later, another woman petitioned Cassandra to sit in the empty chair next to hers, and Cassandra stood to allow her to pass by. The woman was here to see her boyfriend. She pointed out the tall guy standing in the back row. She gave an affectionate wave and asked Cassandra who she was here to see. Cassandra squinted her eyes as she followed the line of Soldiers down the left side of the drill floor where a white transportation flag stood. Just to the front of it stood Brandon. He turned around to call his company to attention. His voice was clear and full of intent. Her heart quickened as he turned around. It was almost time for the ceremony to begin.

Cassandra had been on the receiving end of a mobilization ceremony once before, but never as a spectator in the audience. The view was definitely different, and instead of being forced to stare at the top of some too tall guy's head in front of her, she could see out over the entire formation. She could see Brandon. She could see the other company commanders and the staff. She could see the faces of loved ones prepping for departure. Cassandra imagined the demobilization ceremony to be the same, except with more smiling faces.

Even as she stood on the threshold of deployment eve, Cassandra was still unsure of how she would react to Brandon's departure. Fundamentally she knew he was leaving. She knew she would wake up tomorrow and he would be on his way to Ft. Bliss, TX. She knew it would be the better part of a year before she saw him again, and would need to deal with each day as it came. What she didn't know was how she would busy herself after the ceremony was over since Brandon nixed plans for their final rendezvous. She would leave the ceremony empty handed. She felt the outline of the envelope in her coat pocket. At least Brandon would have one last parting gift.

Cassandra listened as each speaker offered their well wishes to the Soldiers deploying and for their speedy return. What she wouldn't give to be by his side during this next year. The mission only called for one Captain and Brandon was already one officer over grade. The only place she could have fit into the deployment puzzle as a Major would have been Kosovo; a position Cassandra was offered twice before the state ruled against sending any more full time staff. The news initially upset her, but by the time the position was rescinded a second time,

Cassandra was fully ready to assume her role as a single parent. Kosovo wouldn't be in the cards for her, and staying home to stabilize the lives of her and her kids seemed like the better option. Kosovo and Qatar didn't exactly line up either. While both were nine months in country, they were on alternate ends of the calendar. A year was one thing, but 18 months was something entirely different. The Kosovo cancellation reminded Cassandra that maybe God did answer her prayers from time to time.

The Army Song played to signal the end of the ceremony as Cassandra surveyed the clearest path down to the drill floor. She wove her way through the sea of humanity separating her from Brandon. She stopped to hug a few Soldiers that she considered to be friends, and continued to scan her sector for signs of her favorite logistician. She made it all the way to the double doors before turning around to start her upstream ascent.

She spotted him almost as soon as she started to reengage the crowd. He was walking past her in the opposite direction. Cassandra called out his name and waved a hand. Brandon turned his head mid-step at the sound of her voice and rotated towards her like a magnet. He greeted her with a Brandon Fletcher signature smile and asked how her day was going. Without bothering to listen to anything he said, Cassandra buried her face deep in his chest. His whole body enveloped her and in that moment, his fear of public affection disappeared. He was hugging her, in front of everyone.

Cassandra reached in her pocket and pulled out her letter. "I wrote this for you. You don't have to read it now. You can take it and read it whenever."

Brandon grinned back at her as he took the letter from her hand. "Thanks." His hotness killed her.

They both shared a chuckle as she recounted the story of the mobilization ceremony that almost never was. Brandon looked at her with a familiar softness while she soaked in his presence. Just then her mind was drawn back to the reason for his cancelled plans; he was leaving and this was the only day his friend could help him move out of his apartment. Cassandra frowned. She didn't want to stand in his way, but she didn't want him to go either. Her mood turned somber. This was really it.

Cassandra buried her mounting desperation into a hug before it had a chance to spill over. Perhaps sensing her sadness, Brandon held onto her tightly, showing no hurry to send her on her way. "I'll miss you," she breathed into his freshly laundered uniform.

"I'll be back," he stated and smiled at her as only he knew how.

"I know," Cassandra conceded. The weight of his pending departure pulled on her heartstrings. This was really it. He would go on his way and do great things and she would go home to a life without him. She wanted him to stay, but she knew she couldn't stop him. Cassandra wasn't sure she would be able to let him go, but she had to try. She stepped back, and once a safe distance away from him, stated, "I'll see you later."

Brandon took a step towards her then stopped. In his heart he knew what she was trying to do and would let her do it. With a "See ya," Cassandra turned around and let him disappear into the crowd.

Cassandra was torn between desperation and acceptance. She didn't know whether to laugh or cry as she walked away. In her heart she felt like she did her due diligence to Brandon. Now all that was left was getting herself from the ceremony to her truck and back home again.

Refreshments were being offered in the lobby, but Cassandra turned her face away, realizing cake wouldn't make anything better. She watched as couples embraced and families shared in stories. Many individuals and families had plans on how they would spend their final moments. Some would take an overnight trip, while others would commemorate the evening with a barbeque or other festive celebration. Still others only wanted the night air for company. Everyone was squeezing the last bit of joy out of those final few moments. Cassandra wondered if she had given up too soon. She wondered if there were still some final moments left in Brandon.

She made a deal with God. She would enter the auditorium and do one last sweep of the drill hall, and if it was God's will that she see Brandon, Cassandra asked that He put Brandon on her path. She wasn't going to launch a search party especially for him, but if she did find him, she would take it as a sign that they were meant to share one last pre-deployment moment. They shook on the agreement, and Cassandra entered the drill floor as promised. Moments later, she headed back towards her truck, convinced that her first impressions were often the best. In her mind, she had already let Brandon go. She just needed her heart to catch up.

***

Cassandra stared at her computer screen as the cursor danced against the white background. Why did operations orders have to be so hard, she wondered? She was support operations, surely writing a true operations order wasn't far from what she was already doing. If logistics was her job, then all she had to do was give it a voice. It was just trying to figure out what she wanted it to say that was the hard part.

Cassandra often thought of logistics like a ship sailing across the ocean, and it was her job to get it from one end of the shore to the other. She pointed the helm and steered towards her destination. She held on tightly as pieces began to fly overhead. First it was a sail, and then a rudder, then soon the mast began to crack. No replacements parts were set to arrive, but somehow she had to make it with her skeleton crew and limited resources to the shores of redeployment. Every wave that battered the ship left her reaching for another pail of water and someone to hand the oars to. Driving a dilapidated shift was how Cassandra felt most days.

There had been monumental turn over, and most of the people she cared about had deployed, retired or moved on. Change wasn't necessarily a bad thing, except that the change had happened all at once, and most days Cassandra felt like she was barely keeping the ship afloat. She wasn't the Battalion Commander or even the Executive Officer. It wasn't even her job to drive any of the ships, but with all the comings and goings from the battalion, she was one of the few people that still knew how to maneuver it through the water. Brandon needed somewhere to come back to; even if he didn't plan to stay at the Support Battalion. She needed to hold the ship together long enough for him to climb aboard. She would ensure he and his successor at least had somewhere to stand.

Army doctrine was the price she paid to help set the post deployment stage. Being fenced into a particular process and specialized jargon was not her thing. If it meant that the battalion would be better off for her efforts, then she would make the sacrifice. Diving into regular operations also meant increased interaction with the Executive Officer. She required a separate operations order just to figure out how to navigate her opinionated exterior, and time spent with the XO was not something Cassandra cherished.

Diving into operations also meant less time for Cassandra to work on her story. Not that she considered work to be a vacation from responsibility or a chance to serve her own purposes. She was diligent in completing all tasks assigned to her, and often suffered from the stress of meeting her own self-imposed deadlines. At the end of the day, she always met her mission; her mission just now consisted of less creativity and more subjectivity. And as a result, Cassandra's creative processes were often stifled, with her story lacking believability and originality.

That was another problem; her story. While she crept closer to her goal, she was still 10,000 words away. She hadn't written in several days and the December 18th deadline was rapidly approaching. With the holidays right around the corner, she wasn't sure how feasible her new benchmark would be. For being a slow tempo time of year, Cassandra often felt the pressure rising to pre-deployment levels. It didn't have to be this challenging. Battalion was making it tough on her, and she was likely making it tough on herself. Cassandra closed her eyes. She took a breath and tried to imagine what life would be like in a month or two.

She would have made it through the craziness of next year's military planning session. She would have renewed her lease with her rental agency. She would be on the back end of a tropical vacation with the kids. And if she played her cards right, she could be on the receiving end of a vocal jazz ensemble at her local community college. Cassandra glanced at her plans list. Continuing boxing classes and attending her church's Growth Groups were staples. Rolling over her IRA and leasing a vehicle also topped the charts.

She was still recovering from December drill hang over and needed some time to reset. Cassandra pushed the operations orders from view and focused on her plans for recovery. She was going to get a massage next Tuesday. Monday and Wednesday she would take boxing classes. Sunday she would go to church. Maybe she would take the kids sledding that weekend. Thursday was open. Technically it was the day after her new novel deadline, and technically, she would be able to participate in any task of her choosing. She wouldn't have the kids. She wondered if that would be a good time to ask him.

She still had his number from earlier that year in California, and maybe this time she would use it for a non-ammo emergency. Cassandra stared at her phone. She felt like a little school girl. What if he hadn't meant what he said? She had asked Brandon the same question once before, she wondered what made it so difficult now. But Brandon had been different. The whole thing had been different. She was married back then and had no expectations of anything developing outside of friendship. That wasn't exactly the case now. Not that she necessarily *wanted* anything to happen with Captain Spencer, he was just an option that was suddenly available to her.

Cassandra instantly fast forwarded three months into the future. He had fallen for her and she was faced with the difficult decision to break his heart or give up on Brandon. Did she really want to put herself in that situation? Did she really want to put *him* in that situation? It was a single evening, she reasoned. If he fell in love with her from such a short encounter, she would quit her day job and market herself as a dating guru. Cassandra chuckled. The idea of being an expert in anything amused her.

She had already popped the question to him. The hard part was already done. It was just a matter of finalizing coordinating instructions. It was nothing more than logistics. Still. Maybe he had felt pressured to say yes because they were in the company of others. Maybe he said yes because he didn't want to hurt her feelings. Maybe he had said yes because it had been a long time since he had been asked and he didn't know what to say. He was transferring anyway. Maybe it wasn't as big of a deal as she thought.

Cassandra dialed his number and held her breath. She hoped he would answer. She also hoped he didn't answer. She was bound to deal with the embarrassment that came with asking someone out, she was just hoping it would be later rather than sooner. A mixture of relief and anxiety washed over her as the call went to voicemail. She wondered if she should leave a message. Would it be more appropriate to identify herself as Major Miller or Cassandra? Cassandra hesitated. In the end, Major Miller requested the company of Captain Spencer. Maybe he was at work and wasn't able to check his messages. Maybe she should send a text message. Maybe he was avoiding her and her method of correspondence didn't matter.

After a twenty minute struggle, Cassandra hit *send*. Minutes into her logistics conversation with brigade, her phone chimed. Yes, comedy sounded great, and Thursday was perfect. Cassandra tried to imagine his reaction on the other end. Did he think it was a date or did he simply see it as two colleagues hanging out after hours? *Hanging out*. That's what Cassandra had called it when she had first posed the question. Even still, her anxiety peaked to high school Sadie Hawkins dance levels. Did he know what she meant by *hanging out*? His surprised expression at least indicated that he wasn't expecting it. Adding to her embarrassment was one of his Soldiers standing in close proximity. She hoped his *Merry Christmas* was worth her shame and embarrassment.

She hadn't been on a date since before she met David. She counted on her fingers. That was over seven years ago. She wasn't even sure she knew how to date anymore. How did people relate in everyday life anyway? There was no profile to review and glean information from. She had to rely on face to face interactions. Cassandra hoped her trepidation didn't give her away. She hoped he didn't see right through her. All she knew was that he was surprisingly three dimensional for a tech guy, and he too was divorced. He had a fourteen year old and a sixteen year old. And despite his speckled gray hair, was actually a few years younger than her. He was refreshingly witty and hard-working. Cassandra just hoped that he didn't dazzle her too much and make her forget her focus for the past two years.

***

Despite her unpopularity in high school, Cassandra was becoming something of a dating expert. At least an expert when it came to blind dates. She had easily been on 50 or more first dates just in the past few months, an impressive feat for someone who was starting over. She knew all of the words to say and not to say to make a date successful or unsuccessful, depending on which way you wanted it to go. There was the classic, *I had a good time* phrase that one might say at the conclusion of a date, only to be followed by a *we should do this again sometime* offer if the date really had gone as well as anticipated. The latter wasn't automatic. It had to be earned. Otherwise, a simple *good-night* would suffice to end the evening without further obligation. Cassandra had learned the hard way that not all dates were suitable for a repeat performance.

Brian enjoyed hearing his own harrowing tales and no one else's. Greg believed he was the extra bag of chips that came with the combo meal. Justin's social clumsiness bordered on painful. Scott was too melancholy for her taste. Dating was 50% science and 50% ability to relate to others, and Cassandra was becoming well versed at narrowing down her options and finding common ground. The farthest she ventured to date outside the confines of marriage was two months. That was the limit of her abilities. Beyond that, she could find no way to navigate into the seas of longevity.

She initially dated in the wake of the divorce, but had been single for almost a year. It was time. She perused the pages of *Plenty of Fish* in search of a keeper. Harold didn't want kids. Jeremy smoked pot recreationally. James lived all the way in Newport. Cassandra tossed back her ocean samplings and tried again. Jordan wanted a relationship with the girl next door, as long as she came with a mannequin body. Terry wanted a lifetime companion while he waited for his divorce paperwork to process. Alexander wanted a sidekick on his journey to travel around the globe. This batch seemed to demand payment up front and only wanted to deliver once their needs were met. Cassandra tried again. She checked her inbox. The score was now 20 to 1. She decided to try her chances and opened her net with caution.

Hmmm, it was the first response she had received that was more than two sentences. She continued. He lived locally, well *local-ish*, and like Cassandra, was also looking for a real relationship. From the looks of his profile, all social indicators appeared normal. Some of his pictures were kind of weird, but it was the internet and she supposed it was to be expected. His message was even laced with humor. Cassandra smiled as she hit *send*.

The email banter lasted a few more rounds before contact information appeared. She paused as her mouse hovered over the ten digit numeric code. She had *just* met him. After a year-long leave of absence, was she really ready to talk to someone real? Didn't she need to go on 50 more bad dates before she found someone that would be worth her time? Cassandra supposed that was the beauty of the internet; if she didn't like him, she could always block his number and he would have no way to contact her. She took caution to the wind and cast her net.

That weekend saw a trip to the coast with her pups. It also saw a walk at a local park and dinner at a neighboring seafood restaurant. They even tried out the patio furniture at *Home Depot*. He was definitely different, Cassandra contended. He was a mix of failed social graces and boyish charm. He reminded her of a lovable little scamp who always managed to work his way out of trouble with an impish grin and childlike charisma. She wasn't quite sure what to think about him. All she knew was that he seemed to like her and because of that, he made her a priority. Not used to being on anyone's list, Cassandra sought the advice of trusted friends and family.

Just enjoy it, they would say. *See where things go*. Cassandra enjoyed the attention; she just wasn't sure *how much* she should be enjoying it. She definitely didn't feel that movie magic romance that so often played out on the big screen. She wasn't even sure she was *in like* with him. He seemed comfortable and familiar and reminded her of her ex-husband, at least all of the good parts. Cassandra thought back to the days of first romance and what had made it so great. Her ex had been willing to spend time with her. He had been excited to see her. His family seemed to have welcomed her more than hers initially had. He had made her feel like she was someone important, until he did things to prove that she wasn't. But that was an entirely different story. The man that stood before her now only represented the best of her past. She chose to love her ex back then, just like she would choose to love again now.

He had ADHD, but he seemed able to focus around her. He was prone to throw tantrums when he couldn't find the right words, but Cassandra would help him express himself. He seemed unable to hold down a steady job, but she was sure it was just a slump. He had a host of budding medical issues, but nothing too serious. Cassandra didn't know where this relationship was going, but she decided to stick around for the ride. Before she met him she had been at the height of her spiritual awareness. Her battery was at 85%. She was sure she was enough to carry anyone through.

Cassandra harnessed her energy and pressed forward. Relationships were a matter of will after all. Two weeks turned into two months. She could do this. She would pass the two month slump. Two months turned into four. Cassandra was on her way.

Four turned into five. Maybe if she hung on he could learn to be serious about her. Five turned into an offer to marry him. Cassandra had arrived. He had even gotten her father's permission and everything. Crouched by the fire, he handed Cassandra a tissue for her congested nose. She wasn't sure if it was the fire or her fever talking, but her reply was definitely belabored. As she breathed through her obstructed airways, she turned to him almost relieved, stating, "Of course I'll marry you, David."

Cassandra laid down her pen. That was enough reminiscing for tonight. Why David had come into her mind at all that night was a mystery to her. She had exhausted her storied tales of Brandon folklore, and supposed she had to tell her readers something to fill the remaining pages. Cassandra steadied her breath over a long pause. She thought how different her life would have been if she had never clicked *send*. Even her own sisters had made one final attempt to sway her decision on the eve of her wedding. All Cassandra could think was that the shoes and dresses were non-refundable. If they didn't attend her wedding, the official party would have two groomsmen too many.

In retrospect, she knew she should have heeded their warning. But even her own father had blessed off on the union. Cassandra wondered if he had lost all credibility in his older years. Maybe he just wanted her to be taken care of, maybe that's all any of them had wanted. That's certainly all Cassandra ever wanted for herself. Back then optimism counted for more than legal obligation. She contended the marriage wouldn't fail because of her efforts. Not this time.

Really the signs continued throughout her marriage, she just simply chose not to see them. David picking a fight with her over her best friend Tommy. David following her around the house, arguing with her until she cried. The subtle way he made all of his disappointments about her shortcomings. Belief in his own victimization that no one was enough for him, even her. Cassandra's theater experience carried her all the way up until the fourth surgery. The third surgery was fine. They would make it through, and things might even get better if Cassandra believed enough.

The day after the fourth surgery was like someone had pulled the plug from her steaming bath. She had been like a crab that was slowly being boiled; everyone else smelled the delicious aroma but she had no idea she would soon be eaten alive. To her, the steaming water had been normal, comfortable even. With each passing incident the heat incrementally increased. The stomach surgery. His knee surgeries. Her own C-section. His depression. Financial obligations. Child rearing. It had all taken its toll and Cassandra didn't even notice. Instead she chose to focus on the sticky spots on the floor, the pile of dirty dishes in the sink and the fingerprints on the bathroom mirror. It was all more important. She may not have been able to do anything to change David's demeanor, but at least mild satisfaction could be found in a freshly cleaned refrigerator.

Cassandra had just wanted some semblance of control, yet David never understood that. In his mind, she already held the important purse strings in the relationship, and he was fighting to have a say in the smallest detail. What David never understood was it was all for him. She arranged babysitters when he was too sore to watch the kids. She prompted him to leave the job he hated so he could spend more time with his family. She added to his pile of unused hunting and fishing gear so he could cash in on a rainy day. She left outings without complaint because his stomach was upset. She gave up the promise of any personal time just so he could have time to recharge for the next day's events.

Cassandra gave up her need to be touched and held and to be told how indispensible she was to his life, to all of them. She went to church by herself because he was too bothered to get past his latest affliction. She was the social and emotional hub for her children even though she was barely able to sustain the withdrawals coming from her own emotional bank account. She gave up any kind of a social life or personal interests so she could be home the minute she was off of work so she could tag him out of the parenting round. And somehow it was all her fault. She had not done enough. She had acted too hastily.

All Cassandra had managed to escape with in the wake of her divorce was her faith. Even then she was barely hanging on. It was like she was riding a bull; it bumped, jerked and threatened to send her flying off at any moment. Sometimes the only reason she didn't fall off was because she held on so tightly. God had sent her for a loop. She needed to hold on with every ounce of strength she had until He was able to gain control of the beast. Cassandra waited so long for

God to calm the chaos she thought the best strategy was to just to tie a rope around her leg so even if she did fall off, she wouldn't go very far. If the bull wanted to drag her over tough terrain, that was okay. At least it wouldn't get her low enough to trample her.

Looking back, Cassandra was amazed she made it out in one piece. She was waiting for the day she would die of convulsions from seismic anxiety attacks as David thrashed around every corner to remind her of his unhappiness. He had handled the divorce like he had handled major medical surgery; not well, and looking for something to blame for the side effects. Cassandra was free now. Why didn't it feel like it?

She pondered all of the reasons why she felt like she'd been stuck in neutral the last six years. Surprisingly, very little had to do with David. He affected her because she let him. She didn't owe him anything, and even had a court document to prove she was square. Did she think she couldn't do any better than him? Were her pipedreams too high to even entertain the idea of them coming true? Or was she simply too scared to try and fail? Cassandra crossed her arms. Whatever the reason, she knew she couldn't stay there. Sometimes the best way to move forward was to simply move. It was time. She could do this.

***

Cassandra strummed her fingers along the table and tapped her foot. She wasn't sure she could take it much longer. "Well…" she queried. She raised her eyebrows in expectation. "What did you think?"

He pushed the bound papers to one side and held Cassandra's gaze. He paused and exhaled deeply. The suspense was killing her, he knew she had to have answers. He tortured her again with an audible silence and furrowed his brow. "I like it. But you should have gone with my idea of making everyone think it was all a dream." Cassandra sank back in her chair in relief. Her brother had liked it. At least she had one supporter in her corner. She wondered what a free minded audience would think. It had been a labor of love really. She wondered if her audience would be able to see that.

Writing the story had been especially difficult for her, even though Cassandra was often credited as being the imaginative one in the family. Growing up, everything from inventive money making schemes, to "creative" storytelling, to her tendency to conjure up random characters to talk to were her forte. Even still, Cassandra had often felt stifled. She was living a standard life under standards conditions. Not that she wished herself anymore heartache than was necessary; she just longed to leave her mark on the world. Most of her life she had been afraid to take chances for fear of rocking the boat and having her dreams invalidated. The Army had taught her to push through her fears, while David taught her to retreat back into them. Cassandra constantly worried about being exposed as the hypocrite others thought she was. Finishing the book was a reminder that her passions were still alive and well. To finish a product of her own choosing would have been impossible up until even a few short months ago. She had been in survival mode for so long, she never would have thought herself capable of branching off into something that didn't have to do with day to day existence.

That's what the book had been for her though; it had become part of her existence. Writing made Cassandra feel alive. It gave a voice to all of her anxieties and fears rolling around inside her head. It had allowed her to be honest with herself. Writing gave her the audacity to hope for better things to come. Every day that she wrote let a little more steam off the top of her emotional tea kettle. Writing allowed her to feel anger, injustice and even allowed her to experience love again. To Cassandra, the 50,000 word challenge had been more than making her goal and competing with other writers for the coveted title of National Novel Writing Month Winner; it was about reconnecting with herself and her emotions. She had stuffed so much of it down after her divorce, and writing allowed her vent without judgment, just like Brandon had allowed her to do.

He really had been the impetus for her journey of self-discovery. She started writing because she wanted to write about him and it was her way of connecting with him after he left for deployment. Every snippet, every memory revisited was like a bedtime story. She would curl up with her latest addition and imagine Brandon sitting beside her as she navigated her way through the last few years. Wanting to capture her affection and internal struggle is what shaped her character's interactions. She, of course, had changed the names so she wasn't giving away *all* of her secrets. Not that the universe didn't already know that she had the hots for him, she just didn't want to make it *too* obvious. Someone she knew may pick up the book, she wanted them to at least guess as to who she was talking about.

Cassandra often wondered at which stage of the operation she would allow Brandon to read the story. She wondered if it would be appropriate, or if the amount of sentiment it contained would send him into cardiac arrest. If that did happen, she could always add it to the *Afterward* of her book. Maybe she could save the conclusion for him while he recovered in the hospital. Or maybe she would just tell him she was writing a story, and allow him to read it once she made the *Best Sellers* list. That would be the point of no return, and he would just simply have to accept her story at face value. The people would have spoken and he would be in no position to argue.

What about David? What would happen if he got his hands on her book? Would he have even known that she had written one? He would probably just *Google* search her or send out his army of spies to uncover her latest endeavors. Cassandra often felt like she was engaged in a game of detective; she tried to lay out the facts of her life to present to him in a clear logical manner, but he would poke and prod until he felt like he had caught her doing something inappropriate. If he was already angry at her, a dirty sippy cup at daycare could set him off. If he was really feeling frisky, he would turn something the kids said into accusations of entertaining overnight male visitors with the kids present, because only inappropriate interpersonal relationships could begat mouthiness in toddlers. Cassandra imagined a book listing all of his faults and shortcomings sending him over the edge. Maybe *he* would be the one in the hospital bed suffering from cardiac arrest. Maybe she *would* let him read it…

She walked across the street to the mail box. A Qatar address shown on the outside of the envelope, and Cassandra's heart quickened as she reached inside. It was Brandon. Undoubtedly he was writing to see how all of the personnel shuffling was going. Everything was better with him, even routine boring things like intra office conflict. She wondered what he had been up to.

Cassandra smiled as his cursive writing flowed across the page. She found his crossed out words the most intriguing. She imagined him sitting pen to paper, replaying the words in his head only to find that they didn't match what was on the paper. She blushed at the thought of him rethinking his strategy because he wished to convey a clearer picture to her. Even his writing wanted to make a good impression on her. Despite the low operational tempo this deployment, quite a few of his problem Soldiers had managed to pass their physical fitness test and get promoted, eleven to be exact. Battalion was being stupid and overworking their staff. Nothing new to report there, Cassandra thought. He reveled in her accomplishments since their last discussion, and it made him think about his own plans, and what he would do when he came back from deployment. He didn't want to come back to their battalion. He would also need shoulder surgery and wanted out of the military.

Cassandra slunk back in her chair. She was so focused on getting through this year without Brandon that she hadn't given much thought to what she would do when he came back. He gave no indication on where he would go and where he would live. He implied he had a future path, but did it include her? Were they still going to be friends, or did him being upset about not *being further along in my own developments* reference her unmet desire for a relationship? He didn't think he would be ready by the time the deployment was over to give her what she needed? Cassandra loved hearing from Brandon, but sometimes his conversations only raised more questions. Maybe she needed to write another book to address her new concerns. He had occupied so many of her conscious thoughts these past two years, Cassandra wasn't entirely sure which of her concerns were even still valid anymore. She could find out for herself, but she really wanted him to tell her.

***

It was her eighteen year anniversary. Cassandra sat in revered silence at her kitchen table pondering where she had been and where she was going. She never meant for any of it to happen, she had just wanted a way to pay back her student loans. She never intended to do the whole six years, let alone serving as a commissioned officer and hanging out for another decade. How far would she go? Twenty years? That would at least guarantee her a retirement.

If she could stomach another ten with her full time status is tact, she would share the same benefits as her active duty counterparts. Still it was ten years of her life. She wasn't sure how much she had left to invest.

The Army definitely had served a purpose for Cassandra. It helped get her back on track with her student loans and paid for her education. She purchased a home with her VA loan on two separate occasions with no money down. Insurance paid for David's multiple surgeries without her ever having to forfeit a penny. Both of her children came free of charge courtesy of Uncle Sam. The Army had even allowed her to transfer her GI Bill to her kids for use at an undisclosed future date. For all the pain and suffering of uncoordinated annual trainings and deployment, Cassandra had been handsomely rewarded. The military had taken care of her. It even helped in the leadership and job skill department. But the one thing it had yet to produce was a romantic relationship.

There was Brandon, but that was as close as she had come. Sometimes Cassandra disliked being an officer. Everyone expected so much of her and she often felt like her life was on parade for others to see and critique. She felt this especially true in the areas of logistics management and leadership, and at times felt it carry over into her personal life. No one said anything, it was just their perceptions that concerned her. She wanted to make a good impression. Failed relationships didn't send a very positive message, and Cassandra wanted to limit her failures to the private sector.

Cassandra's phone uttered a familiar *ding,* bringing her thoughts back to reality. It was Captain Spencer. He was home now and would have a little time to rest and refit before his involuntary shift change. She wondered if he would be up for company. She resisted the urge to pester him. They had worked together for the last two years, but Cassandra still didn't really know him all that well. She would stave off the awkwardness for another day.

She knew him loosely through drill, and it was only the last couple of drill periods that they started conversing at any great length. He was transferring to state headquarters soon, and Cassandra would lose the ability to communicate with him through work. She wondered how much of herself she should invest.

Relationships were never easy and they required work, but Cassandra wasn't sure she wanted a relationship with him, or really anyone that wasn't Brandon. *Relationship* was kind of a relative word these days. Really, *date* was just as relative and Cassandra never actually got to go out with Andrew Spencer. They didn't quite make it that far. Her secretary confirmed two days before the big night that they were still on for the comedy show. She received a thumbs up. She didn't have the kids and would Uber to the club so she did not have to contend with downtown parking. Everyone was tracking. Because of her commitment downtown, she even offered to stay late at work for a food and clothing drive for her unit. Her shift was relieved earlier than expected, and it would seem her generosity would be rewarded.

That night she had hopped in her truck and sped across town. If she hurried, she would be able to grab a quick bit to eat, change her clothes and battle the evening traffic with just enough time to appear prim and proper for her pre-comedy show drinks. Traffic moved at a crawl and her buffer of time began to dwindle. 7:00 PM was their mutually agreed upon time, and as long as she was able to make it before then, she would be satisfied. She was three minutes away from her house when she received the message. He would need to cancel. She tried not to let her heart sink. To Cassandra, it was a clear sign from the universe that dating was off limits.

She knew this would happen, she just hoped it was for a good reason. She continued to scroll the length of the message. He felt bad for having to cancel. The anger began to swell up in Cassandra's stomach. His dad was being rushed to the hospital with septic shock and things didn't look good. He was on his way to the hospital now. Cassandra's anger left her deflated. How could she be angry at him while his father's life hung in the balance?

That evening she tried to put things into perspective. She would feel terrible if his dad died the night of their proposed date. If that happened, she would just need to swear off dating completely and become a nun. She had two children though, and wasn't convinced she would be allowed to. She appreciated his consideration to reach out to her amidst a crisis, and her thoughts of Andrew and his dad shifted to prayer. A nagging feeling began to tug at the back of Cassandra's mind. What if he had made the whole thing up to get out of a date with her? Surely he would have cancelled with her secretary instead of confirming. If he was telling her the truth, how involved should she be? He didn't know her from Eve, and she wasn't sure if she had even garnered enough points to be permitted into the personal details of his life. He probably had family there anyways, she didn't want to interfere.

Cassandra's perceptions did not improve as the night went on. Her emotions were a mixture of concern, embarrassment and disappointment. She resented feeling sorry for herself in the midst of someone else's tragedy. Maybe she really *had* been looking forward to spending the evening with Andrew Spencer. Maybe she really had considered it to be a *date*. Then that would mean that she cared about him, at least enough to want to get to know him better. Brandon would never stand her up like that, except that he had, multiple times. Cassandra sank into the cushions of the couch. All she knew when it came to relationships was hurt and disappointment. She wondered if she would ever meet someone who could prove her otherwise.

After her initial shock and disappointment began to wear off, she decided to reach out to Andrew. A bombshell was dropped in her lap, and she needed to know how it would end. He was in surgery to remove necrotic tissue from his lungs and was on life support. Cassandra wondered if septic shock was something people were expected to bounce back from. Recovery sounded lengthy and unlikely. She opened up her web browser. She needed to know what her prayers were up against.

She had apologized for all of the questions, inquiring if it was okay to reach out. Of course. Cassandra knew situations were often fluid in a hospital setting, and made her best attempts to balance care and concern with pestering. She would give him some time to let the situation develop and would check in with him in the morning. She advised he not be a stranger and to reach out if he needed someone to talk to. He didn't, and of course Cassandra assumed the worst.

Yet his father had made it through that night. And the next night. And the night after that. He was able to be taken off of life support and was breathing on his own. A wave of distanced relief washed over Cassandra. She could only imagine Andrew's relief and the excitement of sleeping in his own bed. With his favorable prognosis coming on Christmas Eve, she wondered if his recovery would be turned into a lifetime movie to capture the miracle of Christmas every holiday season.

Over the course of those next few days, Cassandra was torn between wanting to reach out, and leaving him alone to share in these quiet moments with his family. She assumed Andrew and his father were close. Quite the contrary, they barely even spoke. Andrew was there because he didn't think anyone else would be, and didn't want his father to wake up and be alone. Cassandra's heartstrings pulled within her chest. Maybe Andrew Spencer was a little more three dimensional than she gave him credit for.

Her phone chimed in her hand, bringing her back to the present. Whether she intended to or not, she was already invested in the life of Andrew Spencer. She didn't know to what degree, she just knew she had to close the loop on her current level of entry. If he permitted her to go further, that was up to him. She just had to get out of the weird place she had been sitting in since her cancellation. She would ask him. What was one more level of embarrassment, she thought.

His New Year's Eve plans consisted of making tamales and watching James Bond movies with the boys. She tried again. He was available the night before. And yes, he would like to get dinner and drinks. Cassandra threw out two potential times and locations. She got a thumbs up. Confused, she decided to pick the time and place, resisting the urge to have her secretary confirm. She was beginning to figure out a pattern of communication with Andrew. Maybe she could just have faith that he would be where he said he would be. That level of faith would require some serious dedication. She wondered if four days was enough time.

***

"Hey thanks a lot," Cassandra motioned as she hopped out of the neon colored cab and sped across the street. It was 6:15. She still had fifteen minutes. She practiced her consolation expression just in case she had to dine alone.

"Can I offer you anything to drink while you are waiting?" the waiter asked.

"No I'm good thanks," Cassandra offered anxiously. She stared at the empty seat in front of her. She hadn't heard from him since she extended the initial invitation. Her assumption was since he offered no objections, he would come. At least that's what she told her obsessions to keep them at bay. She would let him know she was seated and waiting. She kept her phone in clear view just in case she needed to respond to disappointment.

Two minutes passed, and a familiar "Hey," sounded behind her. Cassandra's eyes followed the sound to the image of Andrew Spencer rounding the table in front of her. Cassandra's excitement escaped through a sharp inhalation. She was surprised at the relief she found as he settled in across from her. She scanned her newly acquired image. He was wearing a wool coat and a button down shirt with slacks. He was clean shaven, his hair freshly cut. He was wearing his glasses. Cassandra stopped her mental tally to make a note on the instant attraction his glasses produced. He was still probably dressed up from work, she contended. His supervisory position was likely responsible for the freshly groomed hair and facial features. The freezing temperatures were likely the culprits behind the wool coat. He probably didn't think it was a date.

The evening was put on pause as he ran outside to grab his phone. Cassandra's anticipation began to build and wondered what kind of evening it would be. She wondered what two people would even talk about on a pretend date. She paused her obsessive questioning as Andrew reentered her line of sight. He apologized for stepping out, and with one quick glance at the screen, he pocketed his phone and turned his attention towards her. Cassandra was surprised how much anxiety she was starting to feel.

"When you said that you and 'the boys' would be watching James Bond movies and making tamales…do you have two boys?" Cassandra offered to get the conversation started. Andrew nodded in agreement. It was a tradition every New Years. Each had a different mother, one he had been married to, and the other the result of a "young and dumb" decision. Andrew Spencer had been married. She wondered what kind of husband he had been.

Apparently the kind to work two jobs so she could be a stay at home mom like she wanted. He was the kind who would go away to his officer basic course only to return to have his wife cheating on him in his absence. He was the kind that admitted his ex was a better parent than him. He was the kind to develop a lasting relationship with his children that fostered their dreams and ambitions. Cassandra stared in amazement. Maybe there was more to Andrew Spencer than the sum of his officer evaluations.

Since they were talking about exes, it was Cassandra's turn to chime in. She could relate to the wanting to stay at home piece. Multiple surgeries and depression altered the direction of her dreams. She was running on empty, and everyone seemed to be okay with that. She recanted tales of frustration and despair, intermixed with workplace and co-parenting frustrations. Cassandra was beginning to sense she had said too much, but couldn't help herself. Andrew was new, attentive, and sitting right in front of her. His face was soft in the glow of the candlelight. He saw her when she spoke. His eyes gleamed with a dash of intrigue and tenderness at her emphatic gestures and enthusiasm. A few times Cassandra even cut him off and he responded with softness and understanding.

If it *had* been a date, Cassandra was sure she had scared him off. The conversation gradually shifted to Andrew's military service and his ambitions for his new civilian employer. He was the cyber security manager for a multimillion dollar company. He had employees of his own, and was responsible for network security for the company. He was kind of a big deal. Cassandra listened as his passion rose for his current occupation and how he expressed a desire to want to do more with his life. She paused. He wanted to do *more*? More was not a word she was used to hearing. Status quo had characterized her life since David came along, ambition was not something she was used to dealing with.

Her face softened as he spoke. He wasn't a bad looking guy. She appreciated him agreeing to go out with someone he didn't know all that well. He was beginning to deliver on all the wittiness and cleverness he exhibited over their training exercise in California. She just wasn't sure where she wanted things to go.

He pulled the bill towards him and studied it a moment. Cassandra stiffened. She reached for her purse. "I have cash."

Andrew laughed as he grinned, "I *never* use cash." He placed his card inside and pushed it towards the end of the table.

Cassandra tried again. "Do you want me to give you some cash?"

Andrew shook his head and smiled a polite, "No."

"Do you want me to put some cash in here?" Cassandra asked as she gestured towards the folded folio.

He shook his head with the same polite response before adding a humorous, "If you really want to, you can get the tip." She would. Cassandra wasn't comfortable eating for free.

The bill came and went and the conversation continued. Cassandra talked herself into a sore throat. She was enjoying the company but needed to pop a cough drop. Her eyes began to droop. She wasn't used to staying up late. She wondered how long they had been there for.

Andrew must have been thinking the same thing, and snuck a peek at her wrist as she rested it under her chin. Cassandra turned her watch towards him. It was 10:15. They had been there for four hours. It was past his bed time, hers too. He lived close by, and if he didn't have work the next day, she would have considered asking him for a tour.

They bundled up for December's worst and headed towards the door. Once outside, Cassandra paused. She wasn't saying this was a date, but if it w*ere*, she wondered what the new protocol was for ending one. She had been out of the dating game so long she didn't even know what constituted a date anymore.

He thanked her for the evening, apologizing again for cancelling on her the first time. He didn't get out much and appreciated her asking him to hang out. She wondered if he was the type to offer a follow on date. She paused. Maybe she would just do it. Sensing the evening was winding down and not sure how to conclude it, Cassandra stared expectantly at him. Andrew stared back, equally quizzical. He searched her face. He cocked his head slightly as if trying to solve a complicated math problem before extending an arm. Cassandra curled up inside of it. Not sure of his hug to comfort ratio, she offered the standard rate before pulling back.

As they parted ways, Cassandra glanced over her shoulder to find Andrew glancing back at her with that same look of familiarity he had given her over dinner. Maybe it had been a date after all. Maybe it hadn't. Would he have spent four hours of his work day with her if it *hadn't*? Wouldn't he have asked her for a follow on date if it *had*? More than debating the status of her evening, Cassandra wondered his significance to her. Was she disappointed it wasn't a date? Would she have felt better if the evening had ended in a kiss? If it had, what would that mean for her relationship with Brandon? Cassandra was the only person she knew that could take an enjoyable evening and have obsessive thoughts emerge as the output. She either needed more distance or more dates with Andrew Spencer to prove or disprove her conflicting thoughts.

***

Cassandra removed the *Trolls* themed calendar from the wall and replaced it with her featured *Disney* one. She originally considered the animated features for the kids, but there was something memorable about *Minnie Mouse* or *Princess Poppy* interrupting everyday life to bring you a special occasion. January. A new year. A new beginning. Another chance to start over. *Snow White* was Disney's first animated feature, surely she would set the stage.

Outside of her drill weekend and unit planning session, January wasn't unlike any other month Cassandra had encountered during the last twelve month period. She originally had hoped to take a vacation with the kids at the end of the month, but David put a stop to that, at least temporarily. Once he knew he had no legal leg to stand on, he dazed Cassandra with parenting time particulars and slight of hand exchanges so that her vacation fell on his time. With change fees in excess of the original ticket prices, Cassandra was forced to move the vacation to the following month. It was only money anyway. And her pride. The money would grow back. The pride she wasn't so sure about. Her friendship with Tommy would remain intact too, despite David's best attempt to derail it with pointed attacks and emotional leftovers. Although February was a better month for travel, she wasn't ready to disclose such silver linings to David. If Cassandra had her way, there would be very little she would disclose to him ever again. As it were, they were parentally joined at the hip. She wondered the likelihood of enacting a transplant.

As predicted, drill came with all of the force of a raging hurricane. The ATMS planning session was equally abusive. Cassandra was disgruntled with the organization, her battalion in particular. All she did was give, and all they did was take. It left her feeling burnt out and underappreciated, much like her marriage. However, unlike her marriage, little rays of hope were sprinkled throughout the mundane and offered her just enough inspiration to make it to the other side. Cassandra braved the trenches of drill and her training conference for the prize that lie waiting on the other side.

Admittedly, seeing him at drill and ATMS after they spent a non-Army related evening together was a little weird. The on again off again emotional attachment to Brandon Fletcher had prepped her well for the change. Even still, she was surprised how giddy and nervous she actually felt. She didn't know what it was exactly that attracted her to Andrew Spencer. He was comforting to be around, like Brandon had been. He was witty and articulate and a little nerdy. He listened to her when she talked and seemed interested in her as a person. He didn't seem like someone to take the initiative with dating or relationships, and for being a communications officer, communication didn't really seem like his thing. Neither was it Brandon's thing. Non-communicative definitely seemed to be her type. She wondered if such initiative could be taught.

Cassandra shied away from the larger topics. Command training guidance, pointers on the new Army Combat Fitness Test and Army sponsored medical evaluations seemed to be sufficient enough for drill weekend. Cassandra did manage to switch gears at some point and talk about potential movie times and locations. She was out of practice and he seemed preoccupied. She was surprised how awkward the shift felt. She wondered if it had ever been this clunky with Brandon.

Andrew made a guest appearance as Captain Spencer the following day for their planning session. Cassandra intercepted him the moment he walked in. She was Major Miller now. She was allowed to do those kinds of things. He shifted his attention to her with a bit of surprise as she approached him. She directed him to come see her when he was done troubleshooting one of the lieutenant's computers. He nodded his head. Moments later he stood in front of her desk.

Cassandra did her best to suppress a coy smile. As much as she wanted to see him, he was here to do work. She offered him her chair and explained the training objectives she needed him to meet. Her eyes were drawn to his blue checkered socks. They matched his shirt. Communication may not have been his thing, but color coordination definitely was. She liked the way he looked in a button down shirt. She didn't like the way he communicated his mission essential tasks for the signal section though. Cassandra was thoroughly confused and did her best to reiterate what he just said. This time it was Captain Spencer suppressing a coy smile. A hint of intimate familiarity danced in his eyes. Even in the middle of their planning session he saw her. A smile threatened to pull at the edges of his mouth as he tried his explanation again. This time Cassandra understood.

As much as she wanted to continue to recount his high sense of fashion, she knew his time was limited. She also knew soliciting dialogue from Andrew Spencer was not all inclusive of her duties as Operations Officer. Cassandra rolled up his input and circulated to the other battalion sections, letting Andrew fade into the sea of fiscal year planners. She wasn't even sure the exact moment he left, but did notice her mood shift the moment she became aware of his absence. It was subtle, yet surprising all the same. Cassandra silently wondered if Andrew Spencer was replacing Brandon Fletcher in her heart. She turned her attention back towards the planning session. She had a lot of work to do in the next two days. She would need all of her mental energy to stave off XO inquisitions and attempted banter.

After two days in the trenches, the end of ATMS couldn't come quick enough. 5:00 PM gave way to 6:00 PM, and Cassandra paced anxiously behind her chair. Her computer was already packed up, her belongings collected and she was ready to grab her bag the moment the presentation ended. Although Cassandra was the acting Operations Officer, they didn't need her. The XO was content to run the show herself, despite needing to refer to others' insight throughout the entire presentation. Cassandra stared out the window and wondered what Andrew was up to. He had been smart dodging this bullet.

"That concludes my presentation Ma'am, pending any questions." Cassandra looked expectantly at the XO. They were both the same rank, yet it was the XO that felt the need to exert her position of authority over others. Cassandra could care less about displays of dominance. The presentation was successful because of Cassandra's efforts. A "No questions" response floated in the background as Cassandra shouldered her bag and headed towards the door. The XO's new soapbox was returning tables and chairs to their rightful locations. Cassandra had set up the event, someone else could clean up. Her irritation was at an all time high. She didn't know why she was even upset about leaving the battalion in the first place. They were ready for her to leave and she couldn't get out fast enough.

Cassandra needed a drink and wondered why she hadn't set the date directly following ATMS. Yes she did. Tuesday was the one day he had plans for the week. Damn him. She instead settled for a night in, pacing the halls, waiting for a call from her Brigade Commander. She already knew she was moving. She didn't need him to rub it in. Her Battalion Commander had taken the bulk of her grumpy demeanor following the initial news the day prior. Cassandra's anger raged at his obscure attempt to tell her potentially life changing news with an aura of smug decorum. It wasn't his fault he was a terrible communicator, still the lack of foresight floored her. Good thing his judgment only affected office locations and not lives on the battlefield. What Cassandra wouldn't give to be in the throes of real warfare instead of self-imposed. Maybe a new start at her former battalion would be a welcomed change.

Cassandra counted the hours until her date with Andrew. She still wasn't even sure he knew *this* time was a date, but they were going to the movies. *Date* was practically written into the script. Unless of course, he decided not to read the script. Given his training needed in communication, it was entirely possible. At least Cassandra would have a few hours in the dark to offer refresher training. She looked expectantly to their evening together.

6:15 PM was their mutually agreed upon time. Rather than brave the longer than average work day and head straight to the downtown venue from her office, Cassandra opted to drive home and take her time prepping for her evening in the comfort of her own shower and bathroom. She was a short timer anyway. They couldn't expect her to work longer hours when it wasn't for her benefit. She gave enough of herself to the organization with little appreciation in return. It wasn't even the same organization anymore. So much had changed, even just during the course of the deployment. Sometimes Cassandra wondered what she was so desperately trying to hang on to. All she had wanted was her picture on the wall. Yet those stakes seemed too high for someone willing to take on multiple roles. Cassandra thought back to a year ago when Brandon told her the Army didn't deserve her. Maybe he had been on to something.

She glanced over her reflection in the bathroom mirror. Her heart shaped pendant hung loosely into her plunging neckline. Her thin leather jacket brought depth and shape to her form without revealing too much. Her hip hugging jeans were comfortable and casual, and hung just below her low cut boots. She splashed a hint of perfume on her neck and wrists. One look at her and Andrew would have no doubt the expectations for the evening.

Cassandra checked the drive time. She needed to leave now if she hoped to make it to the theater before him. Her anxiety began to rise with every solid line on her GPS. Why was the quest for the southbound interstate such an anomaly, she wondered? At this rate she would be lucky to make it on time. Cassandra's prayers were reduced to a single *please let me make it on time*, and *please let me make it in one piece* sort of plea. All other considerations she was able to forego. Just then, her GPS beeped, indicating it found a shorter route that would shave 10 minutes off of her commute time. With a click of a button Cassandra consented to the shorter drive time. Before she made it to her next exit, her GPS beeped again, this time offering a five minute dividend. Cassandra wasn't even sure where she was going. If she recalculated mid-bridge, who knows where she would end up. She pressed on. Moments later her GPS informed her she was arriving at her destination. She had fifteen minutes to spare. *Thank God*, she breathed.

Then as God often did, He decided to take Cassandra on a little ride. All she asked for was to make it on time and in one piece. She hadn't mentioned anything about the time in between. Cassandra's navigation application didn't specify which side of the street her destination was on. In the dark all she could see was the outline of a neighboring *Safeway*. She turned into the parking lot. Maybe it was in the same complex. She recalculated. She needed to go back the other way.

Cassandra's flawed sense of direction took her across four lanes of traffic in the opposite direction. She was arriving at her destination again. She looked on the other side of the street. All she could see was an organic grocery store. She took a turn around the block. She needed better directions. She fired her navigator and tried again. These directions gave her step by step instructions, leading her down a side street. Cassandra's journeys took her to the very back of the parking lot where the neon theater pub sign gleamed in the background. Finally. Cassandra anxiously drove her monster truck into the cramped parking lot. *This should be fun*, she thought. She couldn't believe her luck as she spotted a vacant parking space right up front. There was even enough room for her to back up into the space. Cassandra exhaled a sigh of relief and looked at the clock. 6:12 PM. Sure enough, God had kept His word.

She entered the theater and looked around expectantly. No signs of Andrew. As far as theaters went, the living room style lobby and full service bar indicated a level of trendy she had not come to expect in a movie theater. She blamed the city's hippie liberal culture. Cassandra approached the front counter inquiring how it all worked. He directed her to the *You're in the Right Place* sign hanging above the front register. Cassandra blushed. She took a seat at a nearby table and waited for Andrew. She checked her watch. The time was now 6:15 PM.

As quickly as the moment of doubt crept across her mind, it vanished as Andrew walked through the door. Cassandra rose to her feet to greet him. "Sorry, I would have been here sooner but I had to circle the block three times to find parking." Cassandra smiled. She understood his struggle all too well.

She presented her electronic tickets to the cashier and was directed to their table. Cassandra secretly wished she had opted for the "intimate seating" option in the living room style theater, but it was obvious from the online diagram they would be directed to regular theater seating. She glanced around as movie goers settled in on sectional sofas, recliners and even daybed options in the front row. A couple snuggled on an oversized ottoman near the fire. She glanced woefully at the two foot wide table separating their own chairs. Cassandra lamented staving off awkwardness in place of romance.

Yet, his unshaven face and casual dress made it easy to dive into conversation. His eyes danced with the same level of excitement present at the restaurant two weeks prior. He leaned on the table and seemed to absorb every detail Cassandra laid before him. He listened thoughtfully as she discussed the specifics of her new position, workplace woes and what was wrong with the battalion's logistical footprint. For every workplace affliction, Andrew countered with work related injustices of his own. A smile stretched across Cassandra's face. She was sure she would have to wait a year to engage in this type of witty banter. Maybe the universe knew her type more than she gave it credit for.

As the opening credits began to roll, Cassandra convinced Andrew to move the table from between their seats to the front of them. The two foot gap was reduced to a few inches. They were set to watch a movie on World War I. She wondered how much she would allow Andrew's presence to distract her. She would let the food and drinks arrive before she took any action.

Between animal and human warfare gore, Cassandra took bites of her yakisoba noodles. She alternated sips of her mojito for the truly gory encounters. She glanced over her shoulder as Andrew developed his own drink/dinner battle rhythm. After eating, he sat back in his chair and folded his hands neatly in his lap. Cassandra curled her legs and feet onto the cushion of the chair and contemplated her plan. She needed to find a way to bridge those last few inches. She rested her elbow on her armrest and leaned over. She was still a little short. She would need to lean a little farther. Cassandra could audibly feel her heartbeat as she grazed his shoulder. *Success!* Andrew reached down to grab a drink then leaned back. His arm was no longer touching hers. She frowned and tried again.

The *push-pull, drink-move* pattern continued for two more iterations. His actions were subtle, but Cassandra couldn't help but think he was doing it on purpose whenever she got too close. Maybe he didn't like people touching him. Maybe he didn't like *her* touching him. On one such iteration Andrew turned to her and whispered, "I'm going to get another drink, would you like one?" Cassandra shook her head. Maybe she would move his chair over the final few inches before he came back, then at least she would know for sure whether the brush aways were intentional.

He returned moments later and placed his drink on the table in front of them. Cassandra leaned in to reveal the plot line in his absence. She paused before adding, "You should move your chair over here." A sheepish smile stretched across his face as his chair moved in short choppy iterations towards hers. She tried her signature move again. His response was the same. Cassandra deliberately elbowed him in the arm and turned to find him staring at the screen with his hands still folded neatly in his lap. He either didn't like to be disturbed when watching movies or he didn't like her. Cassandra was starting to believe the latter as she sank back in her chair, arms width away from him. He wasn't into her. There was no need to force it.

It wasn't long before the movie concluded and Andrew turned his attention towards her. "Did you like it?"

Cassandra studied his face. His body language didn't suggest awkwardness or signs of being standoffish. His voice was warm and his eyes were inviting. If he hadn't moved every time she touched him she might even think he liked her. Cassandra scrunched up her face. She was so confused. At last she replied, "It was kind of gory."

A familiar smile peered back at her. "Well World War I was kind of gory." Cassandra put on her coat and followed Andrew towards the lobby.

She paused in the living room. It was only 8:30 PM. She gestured to the glowing fire and asked, "Do you want to hang out for a little bit?" He took his coat off and followed her towards a sectional sofa where she was careful to leave a cushion's length between them. He immediately picked up the drink menu and wondered how to get service. Cassandra motioned to the bar behind them. "I think you go up there and you can bring it back to your seat."

It was easily Andrew's third drink, maybe even his fourth. He was either nervous, or really like alcohol. As they settled up to the bar Cassandra offered, "I notice you seem to hold your liquor pretty well."

A broad smile stretched across this face, "Yes. Yes, I do." His latest request stood before him in a short rounded glass. His drink ordering was much like his computer programming; he used a lot of fancy terms and Cassandra was never quite sure what he was referring to. He had an expensive taste in alcohol. And food. That much she did know. She was sure the bill for the night had already exceeded the triple digit mark, and it was still early.

The bartender asked if anything else was going on the tab. Andrew gestured towards her with his chin, adding, "and whatever she wants." Cassandra was caught off guard with the drink request, much like she had been caught off guard with his willingness to pay for dinner. She wasn't expecting to be treated to anything else that evening. She paused to survey the shelves behind the bar. She was drawing a blank on what she even liked to drink. Her eyes were drawn to the nearby tap and asked, "Do you guys have apple cider?" Gauging the bartender's initial reaction, she quickly added, "Hard cider." There were two kinds. She would take the original version.

Cassandra watched as he filled her nearly twelve inch glass to the very top. She wasn't really sure what she was going to do with the alcohol now that she had ordered it. It was rude to refuse a gift from someone. Her thoughts shifted to the drive home in the sub zero temperatures. She would need to drink it slowly, very slowly if she hoped to make it home in one piece.

With drinks in hand, they made their way over to the couch and settled in. Cassandra honored the original couch cushion buffer, taking a drink of her cider and turning towards him. For the next three hours they entertained each other with tales of dysfunctional families, childhood experiences, personal interests and celebrities. They even threw a little politics and morality in for good measure.

Cassandra noticed the intricacies of his face as he spoke. She noticed the softness in his eyes. The way he searched her face as he revealed facts about himself. The smile that threatened to pull at the edges of his mouth every time his stories received a smile or a giggle. His eyes were bright, his posture relaxed. She began to wonder if he really did like her. He wasn't turned towards her like she was to him, but would turn his face whenever she spoke. He seemed to like her enough to not be repulsed by her. How much he didn't despise her, Cassandra couldn't tell. She wondered if he came with an instruction manual.

Their conversation was brought to a halt by the sound of a locking door. They looked around in surprise. They were the only ones left.

As they walked out the door into the sub zero temperatures, Cassandra paused and offered, "I had a lot of fun." His customary "yeah" seemed to indicate he had as well. She continued. "Do *you* ever ask people if they want to hang out sometimes?"

His eyes grew wide and he inhaled sharply. Momentarily averting his gaze he replied, "No, not usually. I generally say yes to people if they ask me though. I like to say yes to things I haven't done before." Cassandra decided to probe further.

His delayed text message responses seemed to be more of a product of his busy schedule and inability to understand social interaction than they had to do with her. Social encounters were not something he generally planned, primarily because he didn't know how to do them. Cassandra replayed the evening in her head. Suddenly his actions during the movie were beginning to make a little more sense.

Cassandra could see he was visibly cold and asked if he wanted to sit in her truck for a few minutes. He climbed in the passenger seat and his shudders slowly ceased as the heat permeated his body. Talking about her upcoming mediation session with David brought back to mind how much she had talked about him during their first encounter. "I have to apologize for talking about my ex so much last time," she stated.

She was met with that same warm smile that she was beginning to grow accustomed to. "Don't worry about exes," he replied. "It's a part of life. Topics don't really bother me. If you want to be shallow, we can be shallow. If you want to be deep, we can be deep. I'm an open book. Ask me anything and I will tell you."

Cassandra sat back in her seat unsure of what to make of Andrew's answer. It was more profound than she was looking for. She wondered if any of his four drinks were oozing into the present sentiment. He seemed composed and controlled. Maybe he really could hold his liquor. At last she replied, "That's refreshing. Not many people are like that."

Andrew's smile gave way to slight dismay as he looked at the clock. "I have *got* to go. I need to get up for work in five hours." It was 11:30 PM. It would be after midnight by the time she would make it home.

Cassandra would need to take a reign check on his *ask me anything* offer. She instead asked if she could give him a hug. Of course. In one fluid motion, she flipped up the center seat and moved to the edge of his. She put her arms around his shoulders and pulled him close. She felt his coarse stubble on her cheek. Cassandra swooned as she renewed efforts to control her emotions. She wanted him to kiss her, *bad.* Harnessing the last of her self-control, she pulled away far enough to offer him a kiss on the cheek. The stubble brushed her face again and she launched back into a hug. Not sure if everyone could handle Brandon Fletcher level hugs, Cassandra heeded her cautions and pulled away. That's not what she wanted, but she didn't want him to feel uncomfortable either.

"Have a good night, Cassandra. Drive safe."

"Thanks. You too. Enjoy your camping trip."

Andrew offered a parting smile as he exited the truck. Cassandra didn't remember men being so complicated. Maybe she was just out of practice. She felt a gentle pulling on her heart strings. Cassandra relented. She wondered at what moment Andrew Spencer had taken residency there.

***

Cassandra's eyes peered into the darkness. Obscure silhouettes filled the night sky as Heather stirred in her lap and Hunter lay curled up in the seat next to her. Both were asleep now, *finally*. It had only taken two time zone changes and a layover in Atlanta to get to that point. Cassandra let her thoughts drift back to the last eight days. She really had done it. She was amazed she made it through the airport, all of the airports, with both of them and their luggage. Patience was not her thing, but to see her best friend and his family, it was a price she had been willing to pay.

The 6:00 AM flight had been daunting in itself. Cassandra wasn't sure how she would pull it off. She could pre-stage everything except for pajama clad children in car seats. Having someone else drive would be ideal. One large suitcase and each child could have a small carry on with snacks and toys. Cassandra didn't know how she would manage once she got on the flight, all she knew was she would need help on either end of the airport if she was going to make it with her sanity intact.

As predicted, Ester spent the night and drove them to the airport the next morning. She loaded the car seats in the back of her BMW and made it to the airport in record time. She parked and saw them to the ticket counter and to security. Cassandra used her military ID to waive the baggage fee, and was pleased to learn that the same ID would qualify her for TSA pre-check. Shoes and coats could remain on. Cassandra was pleased God endorsed at least the first part of her Florida vacation.

The children did surprisingly well through security. Cassandra attributed it to them not knowing any different. They were told to walk through the metal detector, so they did. Seemingly only Cassandra was surprised they made it out without any detection. Once past the golden shores of security, the side effects of the early morning flight began to emerge. "I want my juice," Hunter whined.

"Yeah, juice," Heather chimed in.

Cassandra retrieved some patience she had put aside especially for the occasion. "Yes, we will get you some juice at the store over there."

Juice would turn into milk, and milk would turn into fancy characterized bottles that children of any age could not resist. Cassandra noted not all children could drink from said fancy bottles, and especially noted the tantrums that ensued when beverages were served to them in anything *but* those containers. It was entirely too early for a meltdown. Cassandra needed a straw. She chanced leaving her children seated in the food court to grab a straw from a nearby coffee stand. Doug was her hero. He saved the day, and likely avoided a meltdown of toddler proportions. With snacks and drinks in place, Cassandra and company proceeded to the indoor play area to burn off some steam before the big flight.

This time it was Hunter's turn to test her patience. He didn't want to go to the play area, he might miss the airplane and he wouldn't be able to see his friend Sophia. Only when Cassandra took him to the window to see the plane still parked outside the terminal did he begin to engage in activities other than moping. Hunter and Heather alternated being unhappy. After they were done, they took turns with the other kids. It seemed to be a popular pre-flight game amongst children their age. It comforted Cassandra to know that other parents were losing their minds too. If she wasn't in public, she wasn't sure how many times she would have lost her temper. And to think, she wasn't even on the airplane yet. The five hour flight was daunting in itself. All she needed to do was get on the airplane, and she could worry about getting off later.

Cassandra looked at her watch. "Hey guys, it's time to go. Let's use the potty then get on the plane."

Hunter's eyes grew wide with excitement, "We going to see my friend Sophia?! I'm so ba-cited!" He clapped his hands. "Heather, we going to see my friend Sophia!" Heather clapped and echoed his sentiment. Cassandra wasn't sure Heather even knew who Sophia was, but she was glad to see them both so excited.

Once on the airplane, they had the whole row to themselves. Heather had never been on a plane before, and Hunter only once, on his first birthday to see David's family back east. Luckily for Cassandra her tickets came equipped with free in flight movies. They watched the silent edition of *Frozen II* on repeat until their plane touched down. The two hour layover made Cassandra a little nervous as they navigated the mega airport. The airport trams and moving walkways seemed to ignite their curiosity, and they hardly seemed to notice the hustle and bustle of people speeding past them to make their connecting flight. Terminal B, this was their stop. The children flew into Cassandra's wide stance as the tram came to a jarring halt. She quickly ushered the kids out the open doors, mindful to stay close behind so she wouldn't find herself on the opposite side of a moving train.

Lunch offered Cassandra the toddler meltdown she feared. It would seem 6:00 AM and no nap was at last catching up to them. The line at McDonald's didn't help, neither did the unfamiliar brand of macaroni at the nearby pizza place. Cassandra's patience began to wane, and all she could think about was strapping the kids back on the plane so they could arrive at their destination. Her friend would at least be there to share her misery. Suddenly getting back on the plane became her only mission.

Even with the time change, the flight to Pensacola still arrived by 2:00 PM. As Cassandra exited the plane with two toddlers in tow, she was greeted by a familiar sight. Her excitement surged as she threw her arms around Tommy. He had made it. They were really here. For all of the fears and insecurities David tried to force on her before she left, he couldn't stop them from leaving. She was among friends now, everything was going to be okay.

Cassandra sent Tommy downstairs to baggage claim while she called David to let them know they arrived in one piece. His text was quite opportune, and she took advantage of the situation to let the kids talk to their dad without the presence of anyone else. Cassandra could tell he was pumping Hunter for information, so she ended the call. They had arrived safe and sound, that's all he needed to know. She was reunited with her best friend and she was on vacation. Things could only get better from there.

Excitement began to bubble in the back seat as they turned in the driveway of Tommy's house. The sudden stop of momentum was their indicator that something new was about to happen. They sprang from the car and deliberately searched each room for a seemingly unknown treasure. Everything was interesting. The outside play structure. The remote controlled vacuum cleaner. Even the potty seats seemed more intriguing. Toys and books took on a new sense of wonder.

The front door opened and an excited, "Hunter!" sped across the floor. She threw her arms around him and claimed, “My dad said you were coming! You’re here!”

“Sophia, Heather is here too. Say hi,” Tommy offered. Sophia turned and waved. She refocused her attention on Hunter.

“Want to see my room? Come on, let’s go!” she called as they ran hand and hand towards her opened door.

“Come on Heather, let’s go!” Hunter called as his sister trailed behind.

“That’s impressive,” Tommy stated. “If it were my kids they wouldn’t even look back. Sophia wouldn’t even notice her sister was missing until she was on the other side of the playground. Good job teaching manners and inclusivity Mommy.” Cassandra blushed. She was never quite sure how to receive compliments from her best friend. He joked a lot, but she knew him well enough to know when he meant what he said.

Dinner simmered on the grill as a freight train full of toddlers sped through the house. They were chasing pretend bad guys, chasing each other and running away from imaginary monsters. Cassandra was sure Heather was only running because everyone else was. At least it gave her a chance to talk. She told her friends about the trip that almost never was and the level of harassment she received on the eve of and in the wake of her journey. If it wasn’t for everyone else’s confidence and assistance getting her trip off of the ground, she was sure she wouldn’t have made it if the effort had been hers alone. It wasn’t until the day before her trip that she even bothered to pack a suitcase. Up until that point, Cassandra wrestled with the notion of even going.

Tommy listened with a compassionate ear as he stated, "Well he hasn't contacted *me* yet. I've been waiting for him. I'm ready!" Cassandra grinned. Only Tommy could make light of a deranged ex-husband. He was always there to pick her up. That's what she loved most about him.

David never contacted Tommy. In fact, after the first day, he stopped contacting Cassandra too. Other than sending a few pictures his way and informing him of the return flight, she received very little correspondence from him. She wasn't sure if he had been talking to someone, or at last concluded making threats via text message wasn't conducive to a joint parenting plan, in either event, he seemed to elect against his primary impulse. So uncharacteristic was his response, Cassandra almost expected to come home to a court summons taped to her front door. *Almost...*

The moonlight peered into the window and Cassandra squint her eyes against the night sky. It was hard to believe that they had spent an entire week there. Never in her life had she thought she would have the courage or energy to pull something like this off. She made it across four flights, two time zones and a week of sharing a bed with two toddlers. She was in the final leg of the journey now, and wondered why she even doubted herself in the first place. Maybe she was stronger than she thought. Maybe she was created for more of a purpose that she ever gave herself credit for. Maybe God really did think more highly of her than she ever gave Him credit for.

Cassandra was reminded that not all relationships were toxic, and it was possible for people to love you without an agenda. Tommy and Susana had opened their home up to her and her children, rearranged their schedules and doubled their grocery bill in order to accommodate Cassandra and her tiny guests. They went to the store daily to retrieve items they thought would make her and the kids more comfortable. Even the idea of a sick toddler didn't faze them. They offered medicine and homeopathic remedies in exchange for sleepless nights. Their generosity astounded her. Anything Cassandra wanted to do, they would facilitate. It was her vacation, they wanted her to have fun.

Cassandra was careful not to take advantage of their generosity. They had interests and demands of their own four and five year olds they still had to satisfy, she didn't want to place any undue burden on them. They were her friends though, and they would do anything for her; a lesson she often struggled to accept.

Their adventures took them to the zoo to feed the giraffes, an indoor bouncy house play area, the park and a Mardi Gras parade on their final night in town. The kids left with an assortment of beads. toys, and memories of a favorable cross country trip. Even still, her friends offered her more; a trip to New Orleans, an amusement park, a beach picnic. Cassandra wasn't sure her kids had the energy for such non-stop action. She wasn't even sure *she* had the energy for such non-stop action, not without nap time anyway. The activity didn't matter so much to Cassandra as the time spent with her best friend. She even helped him plant flowers in his garden and rewire a light fixture just to have some quality time with him. She entertained stories of home improvement and home equity for that same reason.

Her thoughts shifted to Brandon. While the everyday longing had subsided for him, he still crossed her mind. On a trip filled with friends and family, he crossed her mind often. She wondered if he ever thought about her. She would send him some pictures. Maybe she would even send some real ones. She wondered what a trip would be like with him, at least a non-military one. She could see him basking in the Florida sun. Even in February it was surprisingly warm. He could have stayed with her in Tommy's house. He could have relaxed as Tommy and his wife chauffeured them around. She was so much more understanding of their friendship than David had ever been. Tommy and Cassandra shared the same kind of friendship that she and Brandon shared. Tommy was real, genuine and accepted her just the way she was. He adored her kids and only wanted the best for her. He was willing to do anything for her and Cassandra knew it. He was the Cassandra Miller of the relationship; full of life and willing to invest in her well-being. She was more of the Brandon Fletcher of the relationship; appreciative of the sentiment but not sure how to process it because she didn't think she really deserved it. Cassandra stared at the clouds. The irony…

Tommy was the first date she went on following her first divorce. He was looking to meet a Latina girl and invited her salsa dancing. Unbeknownst to Cassandra, they in fact had hit if off, but seemingly only as friends. From the start he had cared about her. It was just unfortunate that she happened to remind him of his sister. But because of that, he considered her family. He even invited her to his family's after Thanksgiving feast two years in a row. He wanted her to bless off on his marriage to Susana, in the same way she had wanted him to bless on her marriage to David. She had and he had. In the wake of her divorce Cassandra learned that Tommy had his reservations about David. He only wanted her to be happy and David seemed to be what she wanted. Again, the irony.

Tommy's only experience with Brandon was through Cassandra's stories. The only image Tommy saw of him was from a military dining out he attended with Cassandra prior to deployment. Brandon remained largely elusive to him, and Tommy often wondered what kept Cassandra interested in Brandon's standoffish personality. Tommy knew from his own divorce that relationships took time and cautioned her to not to jump in before she was ready. He often toted, "It took me a couple of years to recover from my divorce. But you're more mature than me. I say it only takes you about a year." Cassandra had celebrated her one year divorce-ary on the eve of her cross country departure. She was ready for that one year time frame to be done as well.

Maybe God was using that time frame to refine His plan for her. Maybe she wasn't ready. Maybe whoever He had picked out for her wasn't ready either. Maybe they were destined to meet at a large scale military function. Or maybe they would meet over the produce section at *Wal-Mart*. Maybe God had kept her and Brandon apart because there was someone better. Or maybe they both had things to work on before they got involved in that relationship or any other.

Cassandra shook her head. She couldn't pretend to figure out God or his plan for her life. All she knew was that God didn't seem to be turning a deaf ear to her as often as He once had. Every now and again, He seemed like he listened to her, and delivered her the occasional items from her wish list; the boxing classes, a chance to write, a trip to see her best friend; less drama from David; a more fulfilling relationship with Hunter and Heather. Maybe the rest was really up to her. Maybe that was God's gift to her, like a *choose your own adventure* type scenario. She would choose the adventure and if He agreed, she would receive provisions to complete the journey. Cassandra chuckled. She should be a theologian. In today's market she could be a best seller. She could hand out her book on drill weekends. She would make the list in no time.

The plane landed with a thump. Cassandra shook Hunter and Heather's shoulders. They uncoiled themselves from her lap and looked around. "What Mommy?" a sleepy Hunter inquired.

Cassandra stroked his back. "We're here sweetheart. Let's go home."

***

Cassandra pulled her truck into the west edge of the parking lot. A small wave of excitement and apprehension crashed in her stomach. The last time she set foot anywhere near that building was almost three years ago. For all of her resistance, she couldn't stop it. They had moved her despite her plea to the contrary. In the end Cassandra relented, agreeing it was for the best needs of the organization. She slung her backpack and courage over her shoulder and proceeded towards the front door. She was in charge now. She needed to look the part. She hoped at least it was unlocked.

Cassandra walked into the conference room and was greeted by a slew of familiar faces. Some rushed to shake hands, while others were welcoming with kind words and life inquiries. Even those she didn't know were tipped off she was coming. There was an aura of excitement in the air that something awesome and amazing would happen now that she was here. Cassandra didn't know about all that. What she did know was she was an officer. And as an officer, it wasn't uncommon to change positions frequently. And often, you were expected to do your job with little training *because* you were an officer. The Army paid good money to make you a leader, reassignment was often how they got their money's worth. She would single handedly save the war effort, so they said.

Coming off of her last drill with the Support Battalion, Cassandra was expected to jump in with both feet. She had just finished the ATMS planning session with her previous unit, and her new one was set to engage in the same version of their fiscal year planning. It was a big job. Everyone seemed to think she was up to the task, and after working with the previous XO, Cassandra *knew* she was. She was nothing like her predecessor. She would make sure her new audience made the distinction.

This would be her first drill not directly related to the deployment, and Brandon would no longer be the main effort behind her hard work and perseverance. She would be working for people who had very little stake in the redeployment of one of her closest friends. She wondered if she was capable of doing something that had no bearing on the future she hoped to create. Brandon had offered her encouragement on the eve of her departure, affirming she was ready for this responsibility, and the move would give her a place to recharge and move forward. He saw it as an opportunity for her. Maybe she could learn to see it in the same way too. He believed in her, maybe she could believe too.

As predicted, Cassandra endeared herself to the new command team by simply being herself and offering guidance where there was none. She listened to their ideas. Some of them were innovative, while others streamlined ways to complete an already established process. While they didn't exactly fit her definition of the military, they were distinctive units with unique skill sets. Units like the Military Police, Public Affairs and The Army Band. If Cassandra hadn't been to the battalion once before, she would have been shocked that these units existed within her state, let alone within the United States Army. But as it was, they were old hat, ready for new leadership and Cassandra would give that leadership, just as everyone expected she would do.

Cassandra's confidence shocked her as she spoke. She didn't know where the words were coming from.

All she knew was they believed her, and took heart that someone invested in their cause. Her Battalion Commander was equally impressed with Cassandra's assertive command style, and took note on the areas she wished to improve. It would be Cassandra's job to man the full time staff and to advise the Battalion Commander on all matters within the battalion. As Captain Fletcher asserted from her experiences as the Support Operations Officer, she had already done all of that and credited her with running the battalion. Now that she was officially in that role, she simply picked up where she left off; same stuff, different mission.

She thought back to her last unit and the XO's attempt to run the battalion met resistance from all parties. She over tasked and overworked them. She was not leading, and was driving the ship before people had a chance to jump on. She was not the Battalion Commander, and neither was Cassandra. The difference was Cassandra didn't *want* to be the Battalion Commander; she wanted her Commander to lead. Her previous XO fancied herself to *be* the Battalion Commander, but lacked the leadership ability to unite the staff to empower her Commander to take charge. It was simple, but complicated. All Cassandra knew was she had a chance to make a difference, and she had command endorsement all the way to the top to make it happen. Everyone else believed in her, maybe it was time for her to get behind that course of action.

Despite its apparent imperfections, the Support Battalion hadn't been so bad. Being the Support Operations Officer was Cassandra's dream job.

That's where she met Brandon. She wondered what it would be like for him to be there without her. They were a team. She wondered if they would ever work together again. Maybe they actually did need to found that *Center for Logistical Excellence*.

She thought back to their first planning conference two years ago. She had barely been inducted to the battalion before she was whisked away to California to start planning for their brigade exercise the following summer. Had battalion not paired them together in the same rental vehicle, they might not have gotten to know each other, at least outside the bounds of logistics management, and at least not right away. Throughout the trip Cassandra was struck by his amount of personal revelations. She barely knew him, and wondered what would prompt him to share such intimate experiences.

The more he talked, the more Cassandra realized he didn't have many people he would consider friends. She wasn't even sure he had faith in anything outside of himself, and God seemed to be largely elusive in his life. Her heart softened towards him in that moment and she decided to do everything she could to let him know he had an ally. The feeling must have been mutual because he became Cassandra's companion the rest of the trip. Everywhere she went he followed. It was like they were joined at the hip. He sat next to her at the conference table, leaning in every few minutes to ask her questions he thought she knew the answer to. He stood by her side as she garnered support amongst her fellow logisticians for the task that lied ahead. He endured hours of mind numbing briefs just so they could have dinner together when she was done. He even followed her through the security gate at the airport all the way to their final destination. Cassandra thought their joint partnership was over once they reached home station.

Yet it seemed it was only the beginning. From the airport, they rolled right in to drill weekend. Their eyes met across the crowded drill floor and Cassandra felt compelled to go talk to him. The way over was paved with various logistics support conversations, and as she moved in his direction, she became keenly aware of his gaze throughout her discussions. Each time she finished an exchange she would look up to find him already glancing in her direction. Their circles of conversation eventually converged and soon they stood within mere feet of each another.

An image of a middle school dance floor flashed across her mind. She shook the thoughts from her head and directed her attention to his upcoming maintenance inspection. She was willing to offer a pre-maintenance visit, and would need to know dates and types of assistance needed. Dates were going fast and he needed to reserve his before they were all gone. She would be available throughout the weekend if he needed to get back to her.

She saw him several times that drill. She didn't know if she was imagining things, or if he really was lingering until she saw him. Once spotted, he would recite whatever logistical shortfall he thought she would be interested in hearing, and patiently waited for her response and guidance. The next day he saw her kids and husband for the first time. Their paths did not cross again until the serving line at their holiday meal. There was no lingering this time, just averted eye contact and lowered voices.

After drill, Cassandra packed her bags to head out to the logistics conference on the coast. Brandon mentioned he had some questions regarding the ammunition for the exercise. She walked over to his area, and waited as one of his Soldiers went to retrieve him. Her eyes were drawn to the brass buttons neatly fastened across his chest. They followed his tapered hemline across his shoulders and down the length of his torso. She held her breath a moment to regroup. Marveling at his professional appearance was not why she came.

Brandon met her with a shy smile and a brightness to his eyes that was new. It's like he was soaking her in, and Cassandra noticed his face beginning to soften. The mental reboot was so subtle he probably thought she didn't notice. He gave a series of minute head shakes whenever she prompted a question. Cassandra equated it to Brandon telling himself not to say what had just popped into his mind. After a few non-committal shakes, Captain Fletcher was back, and no, he didn't have any additional questions. If she could find out how the ammo would be distributed for the exercise that would be helpful in his planning process.

Armed with the latest ammo updates, Cassandra asked if she could call him later to discuss the specifics. He replied immediately to her text message, and yes, he would be available at 6:30 PM. Cassandra's heart quickened as she dialed his number. Why did she feel like she was in high school again? She had a real reason for calling him. It was like talking to the Captain of the Football team. Unlike high school however, the Captain of the Football team actually answered the phone and engaged her in conversation for over an hour. He text her nearly an hour after their phone call just to let her know he was looking forward to working with her. Cassandra sat in reverent silence as she wondered if she just made friends with the most popular guy in school. No. It was probably all in her head.

Looking back, their connection was real, even in the beginning. He always loved her, even before he knew he could have her. Maybe she had it all wrong this entire time. Maybe she didn't need to win his affection, maybe she just needed to notice the times when she already had. Cassandra surveyed her surroundings. Nothing had changed, yet everything was different. Every place she went carried a little piece of him, even the places he hadn't been. She silently wondered where their future would take them, and what form Brandon would take when he got there.

***

Heather stood on her tiptoes as she flipped the pages of the Disney themed calendar, straining to see the images underneath her pressed hand. As *Rapunzel's* face appeared between her fingers she excitedly claimed, "Is my bur day!" It was two weeks away. They were standing on the threshold of May, and Cassandra had no idea how she had gotten there.

Of course there had been the new unit, complete with its ATMS planning session, Yearly Training

Brief and various meetings that seemed to occupy most of her time. Both she and the children had battled multiple bouts of illness since returning from Florida that February. Then there was the new car, new normal and longing for Brandon. Her world was changing and she couldn't even share it with one of her closest friends.

At first the new normal consisted of balancing her southbound commute against the confines of daycare, with traffic patterns and workout schedules shuffled in. Next came the limits on social gatherings. Schools were next to close. Churches followed suit, then boxing, then parks, then restaurants. Essential functions such as grocery stores and banks remained open, but with new "social distancing" measures in place to prevent the spread of germs. Cassandra didn't see the virus as any different as any other cold and flu strains that had torn their way through the country at any given time, yet this one seemed to take hold of people's fear.

That fear led to large corporations shutting their doors or mandating their employees to conduct online business transactions. Other "essential" business ordered their employees to telework, only leaving minimal staffing in their store front venues. The list of essential businesses continued to grow, as society sought to make sense of the madness. Fear gripped the economy as gas prices dropped and stock markets plummeted. It was like something out of a horror movie, complete with face masks and protective equipment. Throughout the madness, Cassandra wondered just how much of it actually existed and how much was fabricated.

Not everyone wore face masks. Yet the ones that did often wore them incorrectly or negated their purpose by touching them with their hands. Little red squares decorated all public areas showing six feet as the magical distance to stand to prevent the spread of disease. At the same time, new businesses emerged and opened their doors to the public for special "to go" orders or delivery. People were afraid to go out, yet there they were; flooding restaurant drive thrus, grocery stores and stand-alone retailers. They didn't want to get sick, but they couldn't resist the urge to buy a new sweater or a vanilla flavored latte.

The inconsistent paranoia soon made its way over to the military in the form of travel bans and "virtual" drill weekends. Teleworking was not mandated, but highly encouraged. Yet the Governor wanted to activate her unit. They set up a temporary hospital as an overflow for sick patients. They distributed medical supplies to facilities and essential businesses. They interacted with local county and state officials on emergency management plans. All the while, braving the roadways as the electronic billboards shamed, "Stay home, save lives." Teleworking briefed well, but to Cassandra was an impossibility with the enormity of the mission that lay ahead.

The moral outrage with shoddy mission planning kept her busy for a chunk of the outbreak. Being sick kept her busy for another. Although Cassandra was confident she had only battled a cold and the flu at separate times, she kept her distance from family and friends as to not get any of them sick. The only people she interacted with regularly were her kids and her co-workers. They either lived together or worked together. Her circle of germs was small. If any of them had contracted the virus, she was sure they would all be immune by now.

Effects of the virus trickled all the way down to everyday life for her and the kids. With so many places closed, she struggled to find activities they could all do together that didn't result in them breaking the law, or getting anyone sick. The grocery store became their favorite activity. *The Dollar Store* and *Target* were not far off acquaintances. Even getting delivery by a local restaurant became topics of interests. Daycare was operating on an emergency license, and many of the children's parents had either been laid off or were teleworking and no longer required daycare. The number of children rapidly dwindled, and it wasn't long before her two children represented half of the clientele. Hunter and Heather missed their friends and Cassandra's family. They missed the activities they used to do. Their worlds were changing, and Cassandra wasn't entirely sure how to bridge the gap.

She knew less external activity meant more activity with mommy. At first she struggled to find that balance, often spending most of the day yelling out of frustration. As the self-inflicted quarantine continued, Cassandra began to come to terms with her new normal. Life would continue with or without her permission. God had taken everything away piece by piece until she had no choice but to turn to Him. Maybe that was the point, and she needed to heed the lesson. If she could learn to be happy with nothing, she could be happy with anything God chose to give her.

Cassandra continued the online church services and Growth Groups. She listened more and more to Christian radio and looked for opportunities to help others. She smuggled toilet paper and other essential grocery and cleaning supplies to her mother and brother across the glass enclosed screen door. She checked in with her family and asked if she could help with any needed items. She joined the month long Kindness Challenge, extending small acts of kindness to others in her community. She volunteered to put a food box together for a family in need. She reached out to David and asked if he was in need of anything.

He had been decidedly less critical and angry towards her since they returned from Florida, and largely limited his concerns to the kids' wellbeing during the current health crisis. He even brought diapers to daycare on her behalf so she wouldn't have to brave a trip out with the kids. He invited her to celebrate their daughter's birthday at his apartment. She wondered if in fact a new normal was emerging despite society's claim to the contrary.

As Cassandra continued to reflect, she felt herself shed a few layers of animosity towards David. It started with the nightly prayers. She prayed for his health and well-being so he would be able to take care of the kids. She prayed to be healed from the hurts in her own life and find a way to forgive him. She prayed for his financial stability. She prayed God would soften his heart and mend the wounds in his life. She wanted all of those things not because she wanted the co-parenting relationship to be free of conflict, but rather because she wanted David to find the peace that she so desperately sought herself, the kind of peace that seemingly only a worldwide epidemic could bring.

As conflict often did, it brought Cassandra's thoughts to Brandon. She wondered how he was coping with the current crisis, and if it even existed where he was stationed. Her thoughts often drifted to him in the ordinary. As she scrambled to pack a lunch amidst the morning chaos, she imagined herself scrambling to pack *two* lunches so Brandon would have something to eat during his day. As she hastily threw items in the crock pot so she and the kids could have a hot meal after a long day's work, she imagined Brandon pulling up a seat at her table. As she used her precious kid free time to finish laundry, she pictured herself putting Brandon's clothes in his drawer and watching him be pleasantly surprised to find them there when he woke up. After a frustrating day at work, she would hand him a beer and give him time to blow off steam, because she would have known all too well about reaching her limit and needing a breather.

She didn't think it would all be unicorns and rainbows, but Cassandra knew enough to know her home was more of a home when he was in it. More than just longing for someone to take care of, she longed to take care of *him*. And his lack of reciprocal relationships made her want to do it all the more. She would love him with all of her heart, making up for all of those who hadn't. Everyday life with him was beginning to look like more and more of a reality to her. She would even give him a dresser drawer and space in her closet if that meant he would stay.

Cassandra looked at the calendar. Just over a hundred days remained. She wondered if everyday life was within reach for him. If it was, she wondered if she would be the one he would reach for.

***

Cassandra took a breath and explained as plainly and succinctly as she could, “In three days, you’re going to go to the doctor. He’s going to give you some medicine to sleep so he can take the yuckies out of your mouth. You’ll feel better and won’t get sick as much.”

Hunter grabbed his throat. “How will they get in there?”

Feeling a bit like a slight of hand magician, Cassandra paused before replying, “With special tools.” She continued, “Your throat might be a little sore, but you get to have cool stuff like ice cream and Jello.”

An ear to ear grin erupted on Hunter’s face. “Hear that Heather? I get ice cream and Jello and not *you*.”

At least there was Jello. Cassandra wasn’t sure how long this incentive would last, but it would at least get him to the doors of the hospital.

His surgery had already been rescheduled once due to the pandemic, and testing for the new virus was now part of the protocol. Cassandra had no doubt the test would come back negative, since most of the germ factories had closed in anticipation of a viral outbreak. Although it never reached the anticipated level, tests were still being required to err on the side of caution. Cassandra wasn’t sure how he would handle the food and drink deprivation, let alone the recovery.

Cassandra and Hunter were greeted at the door with disposable masks. While she had managed to go the entire pandemic without wearing one, her shoulders sank as she placed the elastic strings around her ears as directed. If she was going to give in, at least it would be for a good cause. Hunter wasn't quite as cooperative, and shook his head like a dog refusing to be led. Cassandra looked to the next gatekeeper for answers.

"He's too afraid to wear one," she stated.

"That's okay," breathed a friendly employee in protective equipment. "Everyone else is wearing masks, he'll be fine." Cassandra advanced to phase two temperature screening. They were clear to enter.

Not used to wearing a face mask, she was struck by how restrictive even the disposable ones were. She had no idea why people would wear them any longer than they had to, especially the cloth ones. While she often mentally made fun of others for wearing them improperly, Cassandra felt herself tug on the nose piece, trying to pull the protective covering out of her eyes and position it so she could breath. This discomfort was new to her. Luckily for her she had no intentions of working out the kinks.

She watched as nurses walked by with decorative cloth masks over their paper ones. Some even had face shields. She supposed if there was a place to practice safe hygiene and behavior, this was it. Perhaps a little too overly cautious, at least Cassandra could understand masks in this environment. It was the grocery stores, stand alone retailers and donut shops that left her shaking her unmasked head.

Clueless to the fate that await him, Hunter kicked off his shoes and climbed aboard the child sized ship. He jumped from the helm into shark infested waters, taking a break to run to the kitchen to prepare his imaginary snack. As he headed back aboard, he was greeted by two masked nurses, inviting him to climb onto the scale to see how big he was. From there they were ushered to tiny surgery cubicles where Hunter would ultimately meet his fate.

Surveying the locked doors and tight quarters, Cassandra ventured, "His dad is here too. How will he get back here?"

"He won't be able to," replied one of the nurses. "Because of increased precautionary measures, we are only allowing one guardian at a time to be present."

That was different than the on phone screening she had received the day prior. Maybe now Cassandra wouldn't have to answer to David's insensitive text messages from the previous day. He had wanted her to leave him alone and not talk to him, and now he would get his wish. She looked anxiously at her phone, wondering why she hadn't received more texts along those lines.

They entertained visitors who offered stickers, Play Doh and electronic entertainment. By the third one, Cassandra wondered if anyone had touched base with David to let them know what was going on. Hunter's dinosaurs clashed in a dramatic showdown, pausing to drink from the bottle of children's vitamins she had brought along for the occasion. Just as their strength began to renew, the fabric curtain flew open and a nurse escorted David in.

Cassandra stood with a mixture of surprise and apprehension. “Dad is going to come and visit for a little while. But unfortunately only one of you can be back here at a time, so we will come get you in a little bit to swap out.” Cassandra grabbed her purse and headed towards the waiting room, wondering how the morning events had played out from the other side of the curtain.

Had David been angry? Did he demand to see his son? Did the nurses go out there not at her request, but in an effort to de-escalate the situation? Or, understanding the current environment, did he wait patiently until someone could usher him back? As messages began to flood Cassandra’s inbox, she was convinced which course of action had taken place.

*You’ve got to tell them to let me see him. This is f-ing ridiculous! You’re always doing pulling this kind of sh*t!* Perhaps hospital reception really was a blessing.

Cassandra watched the clock tick away, wondering if he really would swap out with her. Hunter expected her to hold his hand on the way to surgery and to see her face after it was done. How would she feel if David kept *her* from seeing their son? She steadied her breath beneath her mask and pulled out some electronic Bible verses she had looked up for this occasion. As Cassandra read the words, it was helpful to think what change this situation would bring about rather than her unpleasant feelings in this moment. It would pass, and tomorrow she would wake up in her bed still in one piece. She closed out of her passages and focused on the paintings on the walls.

Moments later, she watched as David emerged from the hallway with nurse in tow. It was her turn. Deviating from the request he made of her the day before, she uttered to him as she passed, “And just so you know, I don’t get reception back there.”

All Cassandra could remember after the surgery was holding his little hand in hers. The blood trickled from his ears as tonsils and adenoids came out and tubes went it. Although the surgery had gone well, Hunter was groggy, miserable and painfully reminded of the hoarseness in his throat every time he yelled. He pulled Cassandra’s heartstrings as he struggled to cough out an imaginary obstruction, while simultaneously pushing her away and pulling her in through tear choked sobs. Blood rushed to Cassandra’s head as she felt her knees began to weaken. She needed some air. Her fingers pulled at the edges of her mask as she looked at the recovering patients around her. Maybe she would just sit down instead. She looked at the patient computer and steadied her breath. She wanted to be there for Hunter, she just needed a minute.

Once her queasiness passed, Cassandra climbed next to Hunter in his child sized hospital bed and held him in her arms. As his coughing persisted, she turned him on his side and fed him water through a straw. The crispness washed over his parched throat and he drifted to sleep in her arms. He awoke only once as they were wheeled upstairs and he was transferred to his overnight bed. Hopefully this would be one of few stops along surgery row. Recovery really wasn't her thing, and despite his allegations, was glad to have David there.

After Hunter was wheeled away to the operating room, David all but offered an apology to her for his behavior that morning. Although he never actually uttered the words *I'm sorry*, Cassandra felt fortunate to get anything that even remotely resembled those lines. He was frustrated and anxious about Hunter's surgery, and the changing hospital procedures didn't help. She got it. She understood. She almost told him not to worry about it until he almost took responsibility for his actions.

In the wake of Hunter's recovery David brought up donuts to share. Handing Cassandra a crumbly cake one, he started to confide that weekend had been tough for him for a number of reasons, including the anniversary of a death of a friend, not to mention a reminder of their first date eight years ago. The apology was so close. Cassandra let his passive aggressive words wash over her as she watched their son sleep. At least they had done one thing right together.

Hunter would go home with David and Cassandra would take Heather. As Cassandra left the hospital to head home, she wondered if an actual co-parenting relationship had emerged from the chaos. It wasn't perfect, but at least it wasn't as full of animosity as it had been a year ago. She wondered if she was just coming to terms with David and his behavior or if things had actually somehow changed. She was still nervous about the future, especially school registration and future relationships, but quarantine seemed to provide a nice break from reality. Or maybe she really was coming to terms with her life and her faith. Or maybe it was just the sleep deprivation talking, she didn't know.

What Cassandra did know was life was not the same without Hunter. While she often thought between the two of them that Heather was the instigator, she found Heather was quite subdued without her brother. Having her by herself was the closest thing Cassandra came to not having kids in the house. Hunter was really the heart and soul of the team, and Cassandra found herself reaching across her empty bed to take his hand. She grabbed a nearby pillow and squeezed it tightly. At least she could pretend she didn't have to fall asleep by herself. Even though it would be a short week, she still wondered how she would make it till Friday.

Her temperament started off even and understanding. Even with two children she was affectionate and willing to meet any and all needs. But after three days of sleep deprivation, all of the good will Cassandra had collected for the occasion melted away with each tear and utter of discomfort. Everyone had assured her it was better to have the procedure done as a child instead as an adult. Cassandra might have concurred if that child could express themselves with real words and not just screams and whines. She might have also conceded if that child followed directions and knew her actions were in his best interest. As it were, none of that was the case. On the fourth and final day, Cassandra felt herself reaching out to David as a member of the co-parenting alliance. She had weathered her leg of the recovery relay, now it was his turn.

Recovery was longer and more painful than expected. It wasn't until the twelfth day Hunter was able to sleep through the night and return to daycare. With surgery recovery behind them, they could finally return to life as normal. With everything around her changing, Cassandra often wondered what constituted normal anymore.

The quarantine had effectively brought life to an end as she knew it. Before her world was incrementally turned upside down, she had often felt like she was idling in neutral, waiting for the next big thing to come along to either blow her out of the water or propel her forward. Once the world came to an end with state-wide closures, Cassandra determined she could either wait for fate to smile on her or take matters into her own hands. The gyms were closed, but she bought a punching bag and starting running again. She even started prepping for the new Army Combat Physical Fitness test with a pull op bar and a set of bands in her garage. The churches were closed but she faithfully attended online and even finished her Divorce Care Group. All of the places her children liked to frequent were closed, but they found new meaning in nature walks, trips to the park and crafts on the backyard patio. Whether normal returned to pre-pandemic levels remained unclear, but she knew enough to know it wouldn't last forever. Just like the last few months had flown by, soon she would be standing on the threshold of fall. September would bring confirmation of her lease renewal, school registration and finalized daycare plan. September would also bring the end of the fiscal year, and the return of Brandon from deployment. While she wasn't necessarily waiting to Brandon to come back to start her life, she was waiting for him to come back to see where she stood with him. And if it was up to Cassandra, she would be standing right next to him…every day…for the rest of her life.

***

Cassandra scrolled aimlessly from one edge of the webpage to the other, not entirely sure what she was looking for, yet confident that what she wanted could not be found in any of the profiles in front of her. She was looking for someone rugged, masculine and self-sufficient. She was looking for someone who knew what they wanted out of life, someone whose traits could be contained in a slim athletic package. Cassandra squinted her eyes as she scanned how many of them had angular facial features, with a handful of them highlighted in stubble. Those were the ones Cassandra bookmarked. She eyed the tops of their profiles and wondered when David had become such a popular name.

Even still, she was looking for *him*, or someone exactly like him. Ever since her unsuccessful venture with Spencer Andrews a few months back, Cassandra came to the conclusion it was okay to date someone who wasn't Brandon. She had given herself permission to date again, she just wasn't sure she was willing to rush the prospects, at least not this time. She wondered what a date would even look like mid-pandemic

Would their first date be a Zoom call or teleconference, as it seemed to be a popular option these days? Restaurants were on the brink of opening up, would they simply order food to go and meet in a nearby park? Would gloves and face masks be required if they were less than six feet apart? Would hugs or a good night kiss be permitted knowing people were still contracting the virus? If they somehow managed to get past all of the red tape, would her schedule even allow for a budding relationship? Cassandra's head swirled with questions as her thoughts drifted back to the curves of his face. So much had changed in the wake of this global pandemic, she wondered at exactly what point she began to come to terms with who she was and what she was looking for.

She used to think Brandon was the only meaningful thing in her life and being without him for a year was God playing keep away to teach her a lesson. She had often wondered if work and accomplishments were the only way she would find meaning and be taken seriously. She was playing catch up financially, spiritually and emotionally since she signed the final paperwork over a year ago. Every day was a struggle as she waited for God to throw her a bone. Then God sent the pandemic her way, maybe not just for her, but maybe a lesson for her just the same.

Everything she had clung to in Brandon's absence was taken from her. Church, Growth Groups, boxing classes, even her own friends and family were now strangers. Gyms were shut down. Movie theaters were closed. She couldn't even escape for a solitary dinner or lunch. Drill even took on a virtual feel. All Cassandra was left with was work and daycare. Both of which she was grateful for, but both of which made her feel like her life had suddenly hit neutral. Day to day routines remained unchanged; work, daycare, rinse and repeat. Her sister had had stomach surgery and was unavailable to watch the kids. Her mom was getting up there in years, and she didn't want to expose her to any more germs than she had to. The caregivers Cassandra had relied on so heavily in the early days had now filed for unemployment, or were only working with a single family. More than simply making it through the mobilization, Cassandra was in desperate need of something to get her through the current crisis.

During an online Divorce Care discussion one night, she came to the stark realization that she had been looking at things all wrong. People got divorced because they made someone other than God the center of their universe. She thought back to the pandemic and all of the destruction it had brought in its wake. God really was the only thing left. Maybe it was time to do what everyone said and trust Him. That night Cassandra rededicated her focus.

It began imperceptibly. She noticed she didn't yell at the kids as much, and when she did, her level of anger wasn't as immediate and didn't last as long. The kids were getting on her nerves less and less, and Cassandra was even acutely aware of times during the day where she stopped to revel in their creativity and innocence. She began to pay more attention to her body and the way it felt as she watched the years of body shaming wash away. She was starting to accept the image she saw in the mirror as her own, and stopped criticizing the faults within it that she felt so many others had cued in on. As her perceptions melted away so did the pounds. Cassandra had lost 15 pounds since the onset of the deployment, and was in the best shape she had been since having kids.

Even her communication with David began to improve. The Florida trip seemed to be the catalyst that launched their co-parenting relationship into doable. The only change he could force was the way they interacted, since Cassandra had decided to carry on in the face of his overwhelming hostility. Their son's tonsillectomy was another milestone. Registering Hunter for school in the light of uncertainty also added structure to their co-parenting alliance. Having input on major decisions seemed to take the sting out of their day to day interactions. David still lashed out and there were days he was still decidedly David, but they were far less in frequency and intensity. A minor quip over daycare exchange was all she received most weeks. A year ago Cassandra would have never thought such a reality were possible. Yet here she was; mid pandemic, and full of possibilities.

Cassandra's thoughts shifted back to Brandon. Her relationship and perception had changed of him this past year as well. While she still thought of him most days and wanted him to be involved in her future, she was less obsessed with trying to convince him of it. She was beginning to cultivate a quiet confidence that he knew how she felt and somehow knew he felt the same. Cassandra was beginning to come to terms with the depth of her feelings for him, and how life would progress even if he chose to remain only as friends. The thought no longer devastated her as it once had, and she instead looked forward to the day when she could again see him face to face. She turned his command photo over on her desk and focused not on his face, but on the joy and meaning he brought into her life. With all of his flaws and imperfections, he had taught her how to love someone with every bit of her broken heart. He was the love of her life, and even if they were never destined to be together, she would always remember him for the lessons and love he gave her in his own way.

An airport scene popped into Cassandra's head as she recalled crutching across the terminal with a sprained ankle and Brandon and her bags in tow. She smiled sweetly as she recalled his voice echoing warmly in her ear that cold Michigan day, later embracing her as she narrowly escaped the winter apocalypse. That same drill he held her in his arms despite her recent trip to urgent care for an unexplained sore throat, smiling affectionately into her masked face. She had also rescued him over an impromptu lunch on the first floor of his office building one fateful spring day, and many times after. The night of the comedy show she couldn't help but suppress a grin as the hottest guy in the bar pulled up a seat next to hers. Friend or not, she was as much a part of his story as he was a part of hers.

She glanced at the calendar. Less than 60 days remained until Brandon would exist in the same time zone as her. She wondered if she could be as direct with him as she had been with her Soldiers at work, or if she would melt the minute their eyes met. The details of how they would meet were still in up in the air, but Cassandra knew her Brandon free time was coming to a close. She was a different person now, she wondered which version of Brandon she should expect to arrive. She wondered if it was a character she had already met or someone entirely new that had surfaced during the course of the deployment. From her own deployment, Cassandra expected there to be change, it was just the matter of change in which direction that remained unclear.

***

Cassandra peered into the dimly lit theater as the usher moved them towards the outline of the chase futon. It was that very futon that had caught her attention that cold January night many months ago, and her anticipation began to grow as she followed her date to the ticketed space.

"Can I get you two anything to drink?" the usher asked from underneath his cloth mask.

Cassandra watched the edges of his mask move and flex with each daily special, and chuckled slightly as she pictured him robbing a bank. It wasn't that long ago that she and everyone else were forced to wear one in all places of business as a condition of the reopening. The only reason they were permitted to be without one tonight was on the promise they would soon be consuming food

"Can I get a Scotch on the rocks please?"

"And for you ma'am?"

Cassandra would undoubtedly need something strong to calm her nerves, but didn't want to ruin the moment with a misguided consumption. “Let’s do a Mojito please.” It was tried and true and never disappointed, at least not in the script Cassandra had constructed in her head.

A smile peered back at her through the darkness as he unwound the elastic bands from behind his ears and rested them on the table. “Thanks for the mask Cassandra. Kansas City Royals, nice touch.”

Reaching for her own multi-colored strings, Cassandra replied, “It was the least I could do, and I know they’re your favorite. Think of it as part of a sort of reintegration kit. Well, that and the reusable grocery bags. You kind of missed a lot this year.” She smiled sweetly as her eyes traced the outline of his face. Her eyes consumed him as she took in every feature. It had been a long time, and she definitely needed a recharge.

Cassandra had no idea what movie she had agreed to, other than it had superheroes in it and stuff would be blowing up. She was surprised he had actually agreed to a movie, it didn’t really seem like his thing. Likely the open bar wielded its own power of persuasion, and Cassandra sat like a giddy little school girl waiting for the hottest guy in the room to ask her to dance. Moments into the previews their food and drinks arrived, gliding across the table in front of them like a well orchestrated parade. Cassandra took a satisfying sip of her drink and turned her attention to her hamburger and fries. She would get to her date, but first things first.

She sensed him studying the outline of her silhouette as she ate, and felt herself wiping her face to remove the ketchup she thought must have existed there. Beginning to wonder if she had somehow overlooked something, she turned towards him and whispered, "Do I have anything on my face?"

He inhaled sharply as Cassandra squared her shoulders to his. He paused to steady his breath and delicately searched her face. She waited for what felt like days before he replied, "No you're good." The Captain of the Football Team was staring at her, and all she could think about was her fry eating technique. She wasn't sure what she would do when she finished and no longer had anything to divert her attention. Her self control had not been tested in months, at least not like that.

As the last fry disappeared into Cassandra's mouth, she felt a familiar warmth breathing into her ear, "Are you done?" She nodded her head. Brandon pushed the bedside table to the foot of the futon, leaned back and crossed his arms. Cassandra's heart quickened. She hadn't made it this far in the script yet. Ordering drinks and food were as far as she had allowed herself to go. She wanted to look over, but was afraid of what his eyes might reveal, or what her eyes might reveal about her. She could feel her heart audibly beating against her chest. If she didn't do something to redirect her nervous energy, she would never make it to the closing credits. She had to think fast.

"How does he know that guy there? Are they brothers?" Cassandra whispered towards her shoulder. Brandon looked at her quizzically. It was obvious from the expression on his face he hadn't heard her. She tried again.

As she repeated the words she felt a hand on her shoulder pull her in. "Are you asking if they're brothers? It's hard to hear."

Cassandra's heart beat wildly in her chest as she nodded her head. Brandon responded, "Yes. They were separated before he came to Earth. They haven't seen each other in twenty years." She let the words melt in her ear. She felt his arm still tenderly draped around her shoulder and let out an audible exhale. "Are you cold? Come here." Brandon wrapped both arms around her and pulled her in close as he continued his private narrative. "That guy there has been trying to get revenge for the past ten years. He doesn't know that both brothers have powers." He could have told her that aliens would be attacking at dawn and Cassandra would have believed every word. As it were, she would need to rely on him for the rest of the plot line since he lost her at *come here*.

She felt the pulse of her own heartbeat thumping in her ear, as Brandon's fluctuated rhythmically in the background. If she were a cat, she would have purred. Her chin nuzzled the nape of his neck. Brandon turned to rest his forehead against hers before pulling back to find her face. Her cheek brushed the roughness of his before offering a breathless, "Kiss me…"

Brandon paused to summon his courage as his thumb tenderly grazed her bottom lip and the edges of her mouth. She gave a half nod in his direction before repeating, "Kiss me Brandon."

He moved towards her and stopped just shy of her lips. He held the tension as she felt his heart beat across the chair. He was nervous too. Cassandra met him half way and offered her own tension. She moved through the anticipation soaked breaths towards an innocent peck. Her lips grazed his cheek before she offered another. She let her lips brush against his as she pulled away. She felt her face being led back to his, as he offered an innocent peck of his own. Cassandra wrapped her arms around his neck and lost herself in his kiss. It wasn't until the lights flickered on that she even realized the movie was over. She looked around at the half emptied theater and sheepishly offered, "I guess that's our cue to go." Brandon held her gaze with a tender intensity before replying, "Let's get out of here." Cassandra blushed like a little school girl as the hottest guy in class led her by the hand through the double doors.

Her daydreams never took her past the lobby entrance before someone always interrupted her. "Um, excuse me Ma'am."

Cassandra shook the scene from her head and turned towards the request. "Sorry to bother you. I know you're busy, I was just coming by to tell you the contracting team is here and they wanted to talk to you about the exercise tomorrow, if you had a few minutes."

Cassandra always had a few minutes, especially if it meant doing something that would make her life easier in the future. Up until now, she had written all of the operations orders, including the one that took them out to this central training area for annual training, the day of delegation had finally arrived. The Battalion Commander wanted her to pass the torch, and Cassandra was all too happy to comply. Something as complex and dynamic as operations orders ought to be shared by others, and Cassandra would have been selfish to keep it all to herself.

She stood up and began to walk towards their battalion operations center. "They're right in here Ma'am. They said it would be quick, maybe 20-30 min."

"Thanks Captain Nicholas. Do me favor and give the other staff a warning order to be prepared to start the class at 0800 tomorrow. They can meet right out here."

"Roger Ma'am. I'll let them know."

"Good afternoon Major Miller, Samuel Kincaid with the 403rd Civil Support Team. I understand you're in charge of this operation?"

Cassandra looked around their staging area. The generators, the trailers, the armored vehicles, the tents, even the very command post they were meeting in had been negotiated from outside units to give them a fighting chance to do a field exercise. She watched as the tractor trailer pulled up to the Ammo Supply Point and loaded up ammunition for the following day's ranges. She stood in quiet appreciation as the cooks prepped the next morning's meal with rations purchased and delivered by their battalion supply section. The satellite terminals were buzzing with activity thanks to an off drill coordination to get them updated. She marveled as a gentle breeze blew through the tent city everyone had been so adamantly against, only to find soldiers huddled around upturned ammo supply boxes laughing and taking bets on who would hold the winning hand in cards.

They had made it to the field without any organic equipment of their own. Cassandra wasn't necessarily a fan of Army camping, but she knew enough to know the value that could be obtained. She refocused her attention on her guests and replied, "I just did a little coordination. And actually…" Cassandra leaned in as if revealing the plotline of an acclaimed thriller, "the real credit goes to that lady over there. The whole thing was really her idea," as she gestured through the drawn back tent flap. "Come on, I'll introduce you."

The team followed Cassandra across the field to the shade of the water buffalo. "Excuse me Ma'am, this is Samuel Kincaid, he's with the 403rd Civil Support Team. He had a few questions for you, and wanted to talk about the training tomorrow. Samuel Kincaid, this is Lieutenant Colonel Matthews, she is our Battalion Commander."

Cassandra bowed out from view as the two shook hands and began to discuss the next day's festivities. Her experience in the battalion this time around had taught her many things. Giving someone recognition who was unable to obtain it themselves was among them. Maybe she really was a logistician after all. Maybe she *had* learned how to be a Battalion Commander as Brandon had so boldly asserted in the wake of her transfer. He would have been proud of what she had done here. He would have been proud of all of it. He had believed in her, both personally and professionally, and it was his confidence that made her believe in herself.

The sun began to set and Cassandra's thoughts were taken back to those warm California nights, seemingly a lifetime ago. As the evening breeze blew across her face she recalled that fateful autumn day she had said goodbye. Belief she would see him again had gotten her through this past year, and she clung to his memory every time life got tough. The last few months, Cassandra's grip on Brandon began to loosen and she slowly realized she didn't *need* him to get through life. She definitely *wanted* him, but she wanted him to make his own choice without the pressures of having to navigate the sea of her emotional uncertainty.

She had lost touch after he left country. She had no details of his return, other than a broad flight window they were expected to depart in. Then there was the out-processing, the de-briefs and equipment turn-in. With the after effects of the virus still lingering, timeline for any of these events could easily be extended by a month. He was truly in limbo, and Cassandra decided to remove herself as a complicating factor in his plan. She did miss him though, and on nights like this, she could use someone to walk her through landmarks in the nighttime sky. She wondered if anyone else was benefiting from his lecture tonight.

Cassandra sighed as she surveyed her sleep area for signs of desert wildlife. Maybe she would just go to bed early. Her thoughts were interrupted as an unfamiliar phone number scrolled across her locked screen. While both appreciative and aggravated with the military's ability to reach her wherever she went, she contemplated letting it go to voice mail. It was an out of state number. It might be the instructors for tomorrow she reasoned, and swiped the green icon. "This is Major Miller."

"Hey. It's me." Slightly disarmed, Cassandra sat in contemplative silence as she strained to put a face to the voice. She shuffled the rolodex in her head before venturing, "*Brandon???*"

"Yeah, sorry about the weird number. I wasn't able to get my cell phone switched over yet, and I didn't want to pay 'international roaming,' so I just decided to use LT Roberts' phone. I'm sure he won't mind."

He was one of her lieutenants back in the Support Battalion. He had always understood the kind of connection she and Brandon had. She was sure he wouldn't mind.

Cassandra let the warmth of his voice wash over her. It had a been a long time. "So what are you doing? Where are you?"

"We're still at the demob site. They told us since we were coming back into the country, we had to stay in quarantine for a couple of weeks to make sure we didn't contract any symptoms from overseas. Three more temperature checks to go and we are good."

A smile stretched across Cassandra's face. It was good to hear his voice. "So next Friday will be your out-processing date then?"

"Hopefully. But this whole deployment has been nothing but unscripted setbacks. I stopped expecting things. It is what it is." The last eighteen months had been like that for her. Cassandra knew exactly what he was talking about. "So what are you up to?"

Cassandra was bracing for more complaints and was taken a little off guard with his question. "Oh me? Just hanging out, living the dream at annual training. And you know, saving the world of course."

"Well that goes without saying." The smile in his voice was evident.

"You know, despite the training area, it's actually pretty nice out here. The stars are out tonight, it kind of reminds me of California."

"Is it hot and dusty and the forests are on fire?"

"Well," Cassandra began as she surveyed their assembly area, "there was a big wind storm that came through and knocked one of the generators over and caused a fire. So in a way, yeah, it kind of is like California. I mean, it doesn't have your soapbox sermons on logistics, but I've taken care of that myself."

"I bet you have!" Brandon's words stretched into a smile before offering a more subdued, "You don't need me to plan. That brigade level training exercise and that pre-mob training was all you. You're a real logistician, I just play one on TV."

Cassandra had always been the television actress. That was her line. Maybe he really had taken a piece of her with him.

For the next hour they recalled memories from annual training, deployment experiences and tips for reintegration into the post apocalyptic world. The distance and time melted away and she was reunited with one of her closest friends. She didn't know if it got much better than that.

She was in the middle of recounting her heroic efforts to save the battalion's annual training management session when Brandon interjected, "Hey Cassandra, sorry but I'm going to need to let you go.

Lieutenant Roberts wants to use his phone, and he's been giving me the stink eye for the past ten minutes."

"Okay yeah, I'll just talk to you later then. It was good to hear from you. Welcome back."

"Thanks. Hey, I did want to ask you one thing before you go. Since there is not going to be a demobilization ceremony, I was wondering if…" Brandon paused to gather his thoughts. "If you'd be able to pick me up from the airport on Saturday."

Cassandra held her breath. She wasn't expecting such a request from Brandon. He didn't like to ask for help, especially from her.

"If you can't, it's no big deal, I'll just ask Jeremy if he can swing by."

Cassandra found her words. "No, I'd be happy to help. We're done here Thursday and come back Friday. What time?"

"My flight gets in at two in the afternoon."

"Yeah, no problem. I'll be there. Be safe."

***

"Sorry I was on the phone so long, thanks for letting me borrow it," Brandon stated as he handed it back over to his lieutenant.

"No worries sir. I wasn't mad that you were on the phone, I was just starting to think that you weren't going to ask her." Lieutenant Roberts paused and met Brandon's eyes. "I mean, you *did* ask her right?"

Brandon averted his gaze. He wasn't one to put his trust in those junior to him, but he had trusted Lieutenant Roberts like a peer, regarding him as one of his closest confidants. He had spent most of the deployment denying it, but LT Roberts could see right through him. Naturally he had to come clean.

"*Sir…?*"

Still looking away, Brandon replied, "I *kind of* asked her. I mean, I asked if she would pick me up from the airport on Saturday."

"Did you ask her to do anything *after* that?" LT Roberts insisted

"No, not yet." Brandon's shoe scuffed a small pile of dirt. "I mean, I figured I could always ask her on our way back."

LT Roberts narrowed his eyes in critique. "Any ideas where you would like to go?" he stated as he crossed his arms.

Brandon thought for a moment. "The new super hero movie is out, and there's this theater by my place that I wanted to try." A smile began to pull at the edges of his mouth before turning into a frown. "Do you think she'll say yes? I mean, I haven't exactly been forthcoming with her this whole time, and I don't want to hurt her. I mean…I just…"

"Of course she'll say yes! She loves you. Don't you know that by now?' Roberts asserted.

"I know she does."

"*And…*??" Roberts prompted.

"And, I mean…I guess I kind of do too…"

"Say it again sir."

"I…love…her…too." A wave of relief and tension simultaneously washed over him as he spoke the words. "I think part of me always has, even when I wasn't supposed to." He had a look of quiet reverence as he contemplated the weight of his confession.

“What’s this?” he asked as Roberts shoved a book in his hands.

“Major Miller asked if I could give you a copy. She thought it would be a nice read on the way home.”

Brandon turned the book over in his hands and smiled as a familiar face stared back at him. He thumbed through the edges and settled on the final page. He knew how the story started, he just needed to see how it would end.

www.ingramcontent.com/pod-product-compliance
Ingram Content Group UK Ltd.
Pitfield, Milton Keynes, MK11 3LW, UK
UKHW040005200726
13854UKWH00001B/55

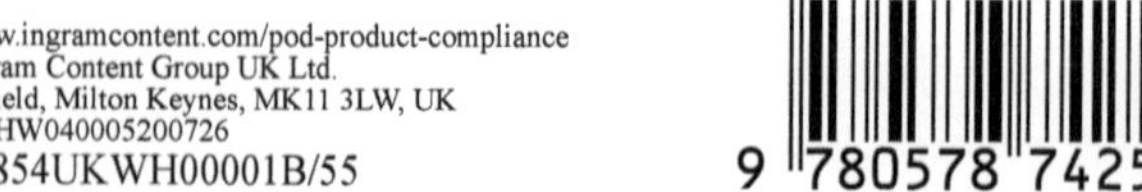

9 780578 742571